There was some innocence in that kiss Ty could barely fathom.

Once he broke it off, she stared at him, her eyes huge. He could see she was trembling. She actually took her fist to her mouth, and bit on it, as if to stop the shaking.

The gesture stopped him cold. "Harriet," he growled. "Harriet Pendleton."

She laughed nervously. "All grown up," she said, as if that in some way made what had happened between them all right.

Ha. She was a friend of his sister's. A kid.

Off-limits to him.

He had to get through the remaining four days without looking at her lips again. Because those were not the lips of a kid. Actually, hers wasn't the body of a kid, either.

Yes, Harriet Pendleton was a woman now. And Ty Jordan wanted her like the red-blooded man he was....

Dear Reader,

Summer is over and it's time to kick back into high gear. Just be sure to treat yourself with a luxuriant read or two (or, hey, all six) from Silhouette Romance. Remember—work hard, play harder!

Although October is officially Breast Cancer Awareness month, we'd like to invite you to start thinking about it now. In a wonderful, uplifting story, a rancher reluctantly agrees to model for a charity calendar to earn money for cancer research. At the back of that book, we've also included a guide for self-exams. Don't miss Cara Colter's must-read *9 Out of 10 Women Can't Be Wrong* (#1615).

Indulge yourself with megapopular author Karen Rose Smith and her CROWN AND GLORY series installment, *Searching for Her Prince* (#1612). A missing heir puts love on the line when he hides his identity from the woman assigned to track him down. The royal, brooding hero in Sandra Paul's stormy *Caught by Surprise* (#1614), the latest in the A TALE OF THE SEA adventure, also has secrets—and intends to make his beautiful captor pay…by making her his wife!

Jesse Colton is a special agent forced to play pretend boyfriend to uncover dangerous truths in the fourth of THE COLTONS: COMANCHE BLOOD spinoff, *The Raven's Assignment* (#1613), by bestselling author Kasey Michaels. And in Cathie Linz's MEN OF HONOR title, *Married to a Marine* (#1616), combat-hardened Justice Wilder had shut himself away from the world—until his ex-wife's younger sister comes knocking.… Finally, in Laurey Bright's tender and true *Life with Riley* (#1617), free-spirited Riley Morrisset may not be the perfect society wife, but she's exactly what her stiff-collared boss needs!

Happy reading—and please keep in touch.

Mary-Theresa Hussey

Mary-Theresa Hussey
Senior Editor

Please address questions and book requests to:
Silhouette Reader Service
U.S.: 3010 Walden Ave., P.O. Box 1325, Buffalo, NY 14269
Canadian: P.O. Box 609, Fort Erie, Ont. L2A 5X3

9 Out of 10 Women Can't Be Wrong

CARA COLTER

SILHOUETTE *Romance*®

Published by Silhouette Books

America's Publisher of Contemporary Romance

To my nephew, Mathew,
(Sarvis the Silent)
with love

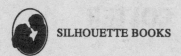

SILHOUETTE BOOKS

ISBN 0-373-19615-6

9 OUT OF 10 WOMEN CAN'T BE WRONG

Copyright © 2002 by Cara Colter

Visit Silhouette at www.eHarlequin.com

Printed in U.S.A.

CARA COLTER

shares ten acres in the wild Kootenay region of British Columbia with the man of her dreams, three children, two horses, a cat with no tail and a golden retriever who answers best to "bad dog." She loves reading, writing and the woods in winter (no bears). She says life's delights include an automatic garage door opener and the skylight over the bed that allows her to see the stars at night.

She also says, "I have not lived a neat and tidy life, and used to envy those who did. Now I see my struggles as having given me a deep appreciation of life, and of love, which I hope I succeed in passing on through the stories that I tell."

Dear Reader,

There is someone I would like you to know. She was my favorite heroine. Ruth Caron was petite and pretty. She had china-blue eyes and sandy brown hair. Her front teeth were a little crooked. She was a playful spirit who loved to dance. She was afraid of water and was always a little self-conscious about her lack of education. She quit school when she was seventeen, got married and started having babies. One of whom was me.

Many of my heroines are ordinary women who reach inside themselves to find the extraordinary depths of their spirits. My mom was like that. Just one example was her terror of water. Instead of surrendering to that fear and passing it on, she made sure my sisters and I had swimming lessons. My mom baby-sat kids to make money, and I think of the sacrifice she made to ensure I would know only joy in the water. In her later years, she even took up swimming herself! (Shallow end only!)

When she was diagnosed with breast cancer in 1990, her courage was monumental, far beyond what anyone would have ever expected of such an ordinary and humble woman. She died in August of 1995 at the age of 57. The hole in my heart will never be filled.

I wanted you, the reader, to at least have a glimpse of this remarkable woman. I wanted you to know, right this instant, someone feels the great love for you that I felt and feel for my mom. Please do breast self-exams and have mammograms regularly. Donate to breast cancer research. Do it for your mother, your daughters, your sisters, your friends. Do it for yourself.

With all my best wishes,

Cara Colter

Prologue

"Your brother is a photographer's dream. And a red-blooded woman's nightmare."

"Harriet," Stacey said sleepily, from the other side of the bed, "Ty doesn't see you as a red-blooded woman. Go to sleep. He's going to have us up at five in the morning, because you said you wanted to see them bring in the cattle from the upper pasture. Your enthusiasm for the ranch is beginning to make me very sorry I invited you. I thought we were going to sleep in, watch videos and make pizzas."

"You can do those things in Calgary," Harriet said, as if her mind wasn't solidly locked on the words *Ty doesn't see you as a red-blooded woman.*

Why would he? Stacey Jordan's older brother, Ty, was the most astonishing man Harriet Pendleton had ever seen. He was tall, broad-shouldered, lean and hard-muscled from years of ranch work. His face passed attractive and went straight to sinful. When his eyes rested on her, dark as melted chocolate, Harriet felt the shiver of pure male energy in the air.

Don't ask, she ordered herself firmly. But a small voice, definitely hers, asked aloud. "Why doesn't he see me as a red-blooded woman?"

As if she didn't know. Harriet Pendleton was well aware she was *too* everything. Too tall, too skinny, too freckled. Add to that crooked teeth, and bottle-bottom eyeglasses. Too ugly.

"Harriet, he doesn't see you as a red-blooded woman because you're my friend. He thinks we're both kids."

"But I'm older than you!" Harriet protested. "Twenty-two is not a child."

"So, tell him!" Stacey said grumpily. "And let me go to sleep."

"Someday," Harriet said, "I'm going to be a famous photographer and I'll have enough money to get my teeth fixed and have laser surgery done on my eyes."

"Harriet, don't be so silly. You glow. Anyone who knows you, knows how beautiful you are."

Except your brother.

Harriet and Stacey were roommates at the Alberta College of Art. Harriet was upgrading some photo courses, Stacey was taking commercial art. Stacey had invited Harriet to spend spring break on her brother's ranch, the Bar ZZ, south of Calgary.

It had sounded like so much fun.

It would have been so much fun, except for *him*. A man like that made breathing in and out seem difficult. Words caught in Harriet's throat. She was in such a constant state of blush that he thought her face was naturally beet red. He'd remarked they needed to keep her out of the sun! She was so self-conscious in his presence that she did everything wrong, tripped over her own feet. After she'd fallen and spooked the cattle, he'd remarked they needed to keep her away from the cattle, too.

"He calls me Lady Disaster," she fretted, out loud.

"He's teasing you, Harriet! Please go to sleep. Please?"

She willed herself to go to sleep. She promised herself that tomorrow everything would be different. And it was.

The next day Harriet fell off a horse and broke her arm.

Her trip to the Bar ZZ was over, ending in the emergency ward of the tiny High River Hospital. At least she had felt his arms! He had carried her, strong and sure, gently teased her out of her pain.

And then he'd said goodbye.

But when she developed the photographs she had taken, she realized she would never really say goodbye to him.

The photos of Ty shone, as if the man was lit from within. She had done on film what she had no hope of doing in real life. She had captured him.

On the basis of those pictures, she was offered a photo assignment overseas.

And on the basis of a badly bruised heart, she took it....

Chapter One

Tyler Jordan was aware he was being watched.

There it was again. The secretary, a woman old enough to be well beyond such nonsense, glanced up coyly from behind her work, looked at him longer than he considered strictly polite and then, with the flash of a secretive smile, looked back to her computer screen.

Ty pretended he hadn't noticed her scrutiny and studied the room uncomfortably. The outer waiting area of Francis Cringle and Associates struck him as being more like the kind of office he'd seen in the rare movie he watched than like a real life office, or at least not any real life office he'd ever been in.

He couldn't believe his sister—a girl born and raised on a ranch—worked in a place like this...actually fitted in here.

He was sitting on a sofa of butter-yellow leather. Another faced him. Huge deep-green plants were scattered throughout. He wasn't sure how a real plant survived in an atmosphere with no natural light. The artificial lighting was muted; the rug, covering marble tiles, looked old and worn in a way that convinced him it had been picked up at an African bazaar.

He heard the quick tap of heels coming down the hallway outside this posh office and felt himself tensing.

If whoever it was went on by, then he knew he must be imagining all the unusual attention he was getting. But no, the tapping of the heels slowed, and then she came in. Tall and willowy, in a tight blue skirt and a short matching jacket, she glanced quickly his way, her confidence astounding, given the balancing act she must be doing on those high stiletto heels, then moved over to the desk and had a whispered conversation with the woman there. The conversation was punctuated with breathless giggles and sidelong looks.

At him.

The looks were loaded with secrets…and satisfaction. Looks not at all in keeping with the muted atmosphere of subdued professionalism that the well-known public relations firm's office had achieved.

Ty frowned and picked up a magazine off the dark-walnut coffee table in front of him. He caught a glimpse of his reflection in the highly polished surface, and it confirmed how out of place he was here. Cowboy hat, white denim shirt unbuttoned at the throat, jeans. He might have raised some of the cattle that provided the luxurious leather he was now sitting on.

A flurry of giggles and looks made him scowl at the magazine, flip it open and read the first paragraph of an article on office management.

He didn't have an office, but looking at the article seemed preferable to pulling his cowboy hat even further over his eyes.

Another young woman flounced into the office, pudgy

and cute, took a long look at him, then flung her blond hair over her shoulder, fluttered her eyelashes several times. If she was expecting a response, he didn't give her one, and she hurried over to the desk and joined the other two in whispered conversation.

Which he heard snatches of. Something about being even better in person, something about people who should be sharing hot tubs and wine on starlit nights, something about crackers in *her* bed. He sent them a dark and withering look that had the unhappy result of eliciting sighs and a few more giggles.

He gave up pretending the article interested him, tossed down the magazine, stretched out his legs and crossed his cowboy boots at the ankles. He looked wistfully at the door.

His eyes drifted to the clock. Five more minutes and he was leaving. He didn't care what kind of pickle Stacey had gotten herself into this time. At the moment he would be no help to his kid sister, anyway, since he felt as if he'd like to throttle her.

A one-and-a-half-hour drive into the center of Calgary. At calving time. Because she had an emergency. Life-and-death, she'd claimed on the phone.

So, if it was so life-and-death, where was she?

And if it was so life-and-death why had she asked him to not wear jeans with holes in them? And clean boots? What kind of person in a life-and-death situation thought of things like that?

Life-and-death meant the emergency ward at the hospital, not the outer office of Francis Cringle.

So here he was in pressed jeans and a clean shirt and his good boots and hat, being giggled at, and his sister was nowhere to be seen.

He resisted, barely, the impulse to send the secretaries

into more conniptions by rubbing his back, hard, up against the wall behind him.

"Ladies, do you have business elsewhere?"

They scattered like frightened chickens in front of a fox, and his rescuer, a tall woman, distinguished, turned and looked him over, carefully. "Tyler Jordan?"

He practically leapt to his feet, took off his hat and rolled it uncomfortably between his fingers. "Ma'am?"

She smiled when he said that. That same damned smile he'd been seeing since he'd walked into this stuffy office!

"Will you come with me, sir?"

Sir. A phrase he'd heard rarely. Usually in restaurants where he was destined to use the wrong fork. He followed her down the hall, having to cut his long stride so that he didn't walk on top of her.

She ushered him into an office, smiled again and shut the door behind him. The light pouring in the floor-to-ceiling windows on two walls blinded him momentarily after the dimness of the outer office.

But when his eyes adjusted, he registered more opulence, and Stacey. She was sitting in a chair on this side of a huge desk that looked as if it was made of solid granite.

"Hi, Ty," she said with a big smile, and patted the seat of the empty chair next to her. "How's my big brother today?"

If they didn't have an audience, a wizened old gnome of a man sitting behind the desk, Ty would have given her the complete and unvarnished truth. He was irritated as hell today.

Life-and-death, indeed.

His little sister had never looked healthier! Her mischievous eyes sparkling, her dark hair all piled up on her head making her look quite sophisticated, wearing a suit and shoes just like all the other women he'd seen today.

"I've had better days," he answered her gruffly, and reluctantly took the chair beside her. More leather. His boots sank about two inches into the carpet.

"I suppose you're wondering what's going on?" she asked brightly.

"Life-and-death," he reminded her.

"Ty, this is my boss, Francis Cringle. Mr. Cringle, my brother, Ty."

Ty rose halfway out of his chair, took Cringle's hand and was a little surprised by the strength of the grip.

"A pleasure to meet you, Mr. Jordan," the voice was warm and friendly, the voice of a man who had spent a lifetime promoting items people had no idea they needed. "Thanks for coming. Stacey tells me you're a busy man. She also mentioned you have no idea why you're here?"

"None."

"Your sister entered you in a contest. And you won."

A contest. Ty shot his sister a menacing look. Life-and-death, huh? Knowing his sister, he'd won something really useless like a lifetime supply of jujubes or a raft trip down the Amazon in the hot season.

"You see, Ty." Stacey was talking very quickly now, catching on that she was trying his patience. "Francis Cringle has been hired by the Fight Against Breast Cancer Fund to do their next fund-raiser."

Breast cancer. How he hated that disease, the disease that had stolen the life from his mother, left a whole family shaken, marooned, like survivors of a shipwreck. Only their shipwreck had dragged on endlessly. Five years of hoping, being crushed, hoping again.

"Okay," he said, not allowing one single memory to shade his voice, "And?"

"You remember my friend Harriet don't you?"

"How could I forget?" Harriet Pendleton was a young woman his sister had met at college and brought home for a week one spring. What? Three years ago? Four?

Usually he couldn't distinguish Stacey's friends one from the other. But Harriet was the girl most likely to be mistaken for a giraffe. Nearly six feet tall, most of that legs and neck, she was covered in ginger-colored freckles and splotches that matched untamable hair. Her eyes, brown and worried looking, had been enlarged by thick glasses. Her quick, nervous smile had revealed extremely crooked teeth.

Totally forgettable in the looks department, not that Ty ever paid much attention to Stacey's friends, Harriet had made herself memorable in other ways. Disaster had followed in the poor girl's wake. She had broken nearly everything she touched, run the well dry by leaving a tap on and let the calves out by not securing a latch properly.

Somehow they'd gotten through the week before Harriet managed to stampede the cattle and burn down the barn, but they had sent her home with her arm encased in plaster.

He should have been glad to see them go, and yet even now he could feel a little smile tickle his lips when he thought of Harriet.

She had made him laugh. And even though he always felt lonely for a week or two after Stacey had been home for a visit, that time it had taken even longer to get back to normal.

"Lady Disaster," Ty remembered. "I thought you told me she lived in Europe now."

Stacey gave him that do-you-listen-to-a-word-I-say look. "She's been back for months. She's the one who had the photograph that won the contest."

"And how do I fit into all this? Life-and-death, remember?" He had a feeling they were moving farther and farther from the point, as if he was being swept away in the current of his sister's enthusiasm. Unwillingly.

"I'm getting to it," she said, her tone reproaching his impatience. "The fund-raising idea is to do a calendar. Everybody does them. You know, the firefighters for the burn unit and the police for the orphan's fund."

"I *don't* know. Haven't a clue what you're talking about."

She actually looked annoyed with him, the same way she did when she'd still been at home and mentioned a film or a popular song or some celebrity that he knew nothing about. She would roll her eyes at him and say, "Oh, the famous blank look from my brother, the recluse from life."

Today she just handed him a calendar, called "Red Hot," which he presumed he was supposed to look at. He flipped through it, without much interest, feeling resentful that he had a ranch to run and was sitting in Calgary looking at pictures.

Very dull pictures of guys without their shirts, in firefighter's pants with suspenders. They looked self-conscious, which he didn't blame them for, and they held a variety of unlikely poses that made their muscles bulge. A few had artfully placed smudges of soot on their cheeks and chests.

"People buy this?" he muttered incredulously. He thought of his own calendar at home. Posted beside his fridge, it had nice pictures of plump Herefords on each month. The Ranch Hand Feed Store gave the calendars away free in December. The Farm Corp Insurance Company also handed out free calendars. Ty had no idea people *bought* calendars.

"Women buy them," his sister said, and he realized it shouldn't surprise him that a woman would buy something she could get free. Women liked to spend money, a lesson his sister had taught him.

"They're especially willing to buy calendars like these if it's in support of a good cause. Like breast cancer research."

Something in her voice made him look up. He stopped flipping pages between March's Bryan and April's Kyle and closed the calendar firmly. He slid it onto the corner of Cringle's desk, remembering, uneasily, all the looks he'd been getting all morning.

He had the awful feeling he had not won a lifetime supply of jujubes. Not even close.

"What have you done, Stacey?"

"I entered you in the contest!" she admitted, her smile not even faltering. "Harriet had the most incredible photo. Francis Cringle and Associates held a contest to find the perfect calendar guy. And you won!"

The perfect calendar guy? Me?

"You mean you set it up for me to win," he said tightly.

"Oh, no, Mr. Jordan," Mr. Cringle interjected with swift authority. "Absolutely not. All the entries were done in a double blind. Your sister was not one of the judges."

"Who were the judges?" he asked reluctantly, not really caring. He slid a look at the door, planning his escape route.

Mr. Cringle answered. "We set up the entries at a local mall for a week. Over two thousand women voted. Do you want to hear the strangest thing? Ninety percent of them voted for you. Ninety percent!"

He felt a sick kind of embarrassment at the idea of that

many women ogling a picture of him. And he felt more than a little angry at his sister.

"The concept we're working with," Mr. Cringle told him, "is a one-man calendar. Different photos illustrating different real-life scenarios that man finds himself in. I was thrilled to hear you are a rancher. The photo opportunities are mind-boggling."

Ty felt he should have boggled Stacey's mind—or maybe her behind—when she skipped school in the tenth grade. And when she snuck out her bedroom window in the eleventh. He should never have allowed her to be so mouthy and strong-willed. He should have definitely drawn the line with her when she had begun to date that hippie. If he had managed to control her in any one of those circumstances maybe he wouldn't be sitting here now.

Now, it seemed it was too late to straighten his sister out. Ty would just have to try and save himself.

"Mr. Cringle," he said carefully, "I'm sorry. My sister has wasted your time. I'm not a calendar model, and I never will be. I'm a rancher. Despite what women who buy calendars might want to believe, there is nothing even vaguely appealing about the kind of work I do. I'm usually up to my ears in mud and crap."

"Oh, Ty," Stacey said, "it's not as if the calendars come in scratch and sniff. Women love those kind of pictures. Sweat. Mud. Rippling muscles. Jeans faded across the rear. You're perfect for the job, Ty."

Ty was staring at his sister with dismay. Women liked stuff like that? And how the hell did she know? He realized he hated that she was a full-fledged adult.

"So, hire a model," Ty said, and heard the testiness in his voice. "If you need some mud, I'll provide it."

"Models are so—" Stacey searched for the word, beamed when she found it "—slick."

Ty could only hope she didn't know that from firsthand experience.

"Mr. Jordan, I'm sure there were male models among the entries that were posted at the mall. The result of the competition tells me women can tell the difference between someone posing as a rugged, raw, one hundred per-cent man and the actual man." Cringle regarded him intently, then said softly, "Ninety per cent is a whole lot of calendars."

"Yeah, well." Ty glared at his sister.

"Mr. Cringle, you leave him to me," Stacey said brightly, but Ty noticed her eyes had tears in them. She'd better not even think she was going to change his mind with the waterworks thing.

It had worked way too many times before. That was part of the problem. Stacey knew exactly how to tug at his heartstrings.

The rest of the world probably thought he didn't have a heart.

But his little sister knew the truth about him.

When she was seven their mother had died of breast cancer. A year later their father had been killed in a single-car accident, though Ty still wondered how accidental it had been. His father had become a shell of a man since his wife had died.

Ty had been eighteen when the accident occurred. Way too young to be thrust into the responsibility of bringing up a little girl.

But what choice had he had?

Ship her off to an aunt and uncle he barely knew? Let her go to a foster home? Not while he lived and breathed.

There had been absolutely no choice. None. His sister had needed him to grow up fast, and he had.

"Why don't we go have lunch together?" she said to him sweetly. "And we'll meet Mr. Cringle back here at, say, one o'clock?"

Ty decided not to lay down the law with her in front of her boss. He got up, extended his hand again. "Mr. Cringle," he said with finality.

But the man looked from him to his sister and back with a twinkle in his eye.

"Until we meet again," Cringle said.

"Which, hopefully, will be never," Ty muttered under his breath as he herded his sister toward the door.

"I don't have time for lunch," he told her in the hallway. "Calves are hitting the ground as we speak. And I'm not changing my mind about the calendar thing. Get it out of your head. It's never going to happen. Never."

Her eyes were welling up with tears. "Ty, don't be so stubborn."

The tears reminded him how careful he had to be about using the word *never* with Stacey. Somehow it always came back to bite him.

He'd said *never* the first time he'd seen her in makeup, reacting to how the inexpertly applied gunk had stolen the fresh innocence from her face. And then he'd ended up paying for her to take a full day of instructions in makeup application at Face Up and buying all the products she needed. That had been about a whopper of a bill.

He'd said *never* to her choice of a prom dress, low cut, clinging, way too old for her, and ended up being dragged into places no man in his right mind wanted to go, for days, finding a dress they could both agree on.

And he'd said *never* to the hippie, which had made the hippie twice as attractive to her, and made him realize that it was no longer his job to say anything to Stacey. Somehow, with so many stumbles on his part and so many mistakes, she had grown up, anyway. Into a young woman who knew her own mind and made pretty reasonable decisions most of the time.

But not this time. "What were you thinking, entering my picture without asking me? Geez, Stacey!"

"It was just a lark. Harriet suggested it."

Somehow he should have known Harriet was involved in this disaster. Harriet and disaster went together as naturally as peanut butter and jam, saddles and cow horses, trucks and tires.

"Besides," his sister said blithely, "how did I know you were going to win?"

He sighed. Was she deliberately missing the point? She was wiping tears off her face with the back of her sweater, getting little black smudges all over the white sleeve. Hard to stop noticing stuff like that even though he didn't buy her clothes anymore.

"Could you take me for lunch?" she said with a little hiccup. "You must need a break from Cookie's meals by now. Besides, you hardly ever see me anymore."

He looked at her. His little sister was all grown up. Becoming more a big-city woman every time he saw her. Maybe it wasn't such a good idea to pass by these chances to be with her.

"Okay," he said grudgingly. "Lunch. But cheap and fast." He was thinking along the lines of the Burger in a Bag he had passed on the corner before this office building.

Of course she took him to a little French restaurant that wasn't cheap and wasn't even remotely fast.

Despite his annoyance with her, she made him laugh when she told him about how she was hiding a Saint

Bernard that she had found, in her little apartment. So far no one had answered the ad she had put in the paper.

"The dog," she said proudly, "knows how to open the fridge."

A Saint Bernard who knew how to open the fridge? "That explains why the owners aren't answering the ad," Ty commented.

The food came. He'd refused wine—wine with lunch?—but Stacey had ignored him and was pouring him another glass from the carafe of house white that she had ordered.

"You know, Ty, Mom died of breast cancer."

He took a long sip of wine, then set it down. Okay. Now that Stacey had fed him and lured him into drinking wine with lunch, she was going to try and sucker punch him.

"I hadn't forgotten," he said quietly.

"Don't you think it's our *obligation* to fight the disease that took our mother? Don't you remember how awful it was?"

He suspected he remembered better than she did, since he had been older at the time. He glared at her, seeing the corner she was backing him into. He said nothing and against his better judgment took another sip of the wine.

"That calendar could make the research foundation a lot of money." She made sure she had his full attention, laid her hand on his. She named a figure.

He nearly spit out the wine. "Are you serious?"

"Dead serious. It's not very many people who have a chance to give that kind of money to the charity of their choice."

"Just because I said I don't want to do it doesn't mean they aren't going to go ahead with the calendar."

"No. But ninety percent of the women who voted liked

you—ninety percent. That's huge, Ty, especially if it translates into them buying calendars. There are 750,000 people in Calgary alone. I estimate 200,000 of them are women. If only fifty percent of them bought calendars, that would be a huge amount of money! In this city alone!''

He could feel his head starting to swim, and not from the wine. "Stacey," he said carefully, enunciating every word, "I'm not doing it."

He avoided saying never.

"Oh, Ty.'' She sighed and looked at her fingernails. "You wouldn't even have to come in to the city. You wouldn't even have to miss an hour's work."

"I said no."

"You wouldn't even know the photographer was there. The photographer's all lined up. World class."

"No."

"So, it won't cost you anything, not even time, and you have a chance to contribute so much to a cause that is very meaningful to you, and you say no?''

"That's right," he said, and he hoped she didn't hear the first little sliver of uncertainly in his voice.

"If the calendar was a huge success, I think I'd get a raise. I'd be able to buy a little house. With a backyard for Basil."

"Basil is the Saint Bernard, I hope."

She nodded sadly. "I think the landlord suspects I have him."

"I'm not posing for calendars so you can keep a dog that's bigger than my horse and has the dubious talent of opening a fridge." At least, he thought, his sister was planning her life around a dog, and not the hippie. He noticed she hadn't mentioned the beau today. Did he dare hope he was out of the picture? Or was it because Ty had lost his temper when she had mentioned the hippie and marriage in the same breath once? He decided he didn't want to know.

She took a little sip of her wine and looked at her lap. She finally said, in a small voice, "You know my chances of getting it are high, don't you?"

"What?" There. She'd managed to completely lose him with her conversational acrobatics.

"My chances of getting breast cancer are higher than other peoples. Because Mom died of it."

"Aw, Stacey."

"The only thing that will change that is research."

He looked across the table at her and saw her fear was real. He felt his heart break in two when he thought of her in terms of that disease. Wouldn't he have done anything to make his mother well?

Wouldn't he do anything to keep his little sister from having to go down that same road? From diagnosis to surgery to chemo to years of struggle to a death that was immeasurably painful and without dignity?

If he was able to raise those kinds of dollars to research a disease that might affect his sister, did he really have any choice at all? If the stupid calendar raised only half as much, or a third as much as his sister's idealistic estimate, did he have any choice?

Wasn't this almost the very same feeling he'd had the day a social worker had looked at him and said, "She could go to your uncle Milton. Or to a foster home close to here. If you can't take her."

He glared at his sister. He saw the little smile working around the edges of her lips and realized they both knew she had won.

"Don't even think I'm taking off my shirt," he said, conceding with ill grace.

"I don't know, Ty. If you took off your shirt, we might be able to sell a million copies of the calendar." She correctly interpreted the look he gave her. "Okay, okay," she said, laughing. "Thank you, Ty. Thank you. I owe my life to you."

He hoped that would never be true.

She got up out of her chair, came around the table, threw her arms around his neck and kissed him on his cheeks. About sixteen times.

Until everyone at the tables around them were looking over and smiling indulgently.

"This is my brother," she announced, happily. "He's my hero."

Chapter Two

If Tyler Jordan was the most handsome man alive, being angry did not diminish that in the least. Maybe it even accentuated the rugged cut, the masculine perfection, of his sun- and wind-burned features.

And Harriet Pendleton Snow knew he was angry, even before he spoke. The energy bristled in the air around him.

"I was expecting a man," he said, impatience flashing in his dark eyes. He looked down at a scrap of paper in his hand, and she caught a glimpse of bold, impatient handwriting. "Harry Winter."

"Harrie Snow," she corrected him. "That would be me." He hadn't recognized her. And she didn't really know whether to be pleased or hurt by that.

A lot of things had changed in four years.

Outwardly. Inwardly she was doing the same slow melt she had done the first time she had met her best friend's brother. She had been twenty-two years old when she had first met her best friend's brother.

Standing right here in this same driveway, the little

white frame house behind them, a larger barn behind that, the rolling hills of the Rocky Mountain foothills stretching into infinity on all sides of them, and all of that majesty fading to nothing when his eyes had met hers.

Dark and full of mystery.

Over the years she had tried to tell herself it was other things that had stolen her breath so completely that day.

The immensity of the land.

The romance of the ranch.

The fragrance of the air.

But standing before him now, she was not so sure.

"I find it hard to believe a woman like you is named Harry," he snapped.

"Like me?" she said. "What does that mean?" Personally she found it even harder to believe that a perfectly rational woman like her mother had looked down at a squirming red-faced bundle of life and seen a Harriet. It was a name she hated and had been trying to lose for years.

He rolled a big shoulder, irritated, gestured. "Like you," he said. "Polished, pretty—"

Polished. Which meant all the hours spent choosing just the right outfit, until her bed and her floor had been littered with discards, had been well spent. It meant that the new haircut had succeeded, for the time, in taming her wild curls. It meant her new hair color, copper, instead of plain old red, was as sophisticated as she'd hoped. It meant maybe it wasn't so ridiculous to try to match your lip shade with your nail enamel.

Pretty. He'd called *her* pretty. For a girl who had grown up thinking of herself as plain at best, homely at worst, they were words she could never hear enough of.

But, before she had a chance to savor that too deeply,

it sank in that he hadn't exactly said *pretty* as if he thought it was a good thing.

"—an absolute pain around a ranch," he was saying. "Were you going to ride a horse in a skirt, or is that supposed to put me in the right frame of mind to have my picture taken?"

Was he crankier than he had been back then? Stacey said he was perpetually cranky, but that was not what Harriet had seen in the week she'd been here four years ago.

She'd seen a young man who had shouldered a huge responsibility, defying the fact he probably was ill-prepared to act as anybody's parent. She had seen he wore sternness like a tough outer skin so his sister wouldn't see how easily she could have anything she wanted from him because he loved her so.

That love, despite his efforts to disguise it, had been just below the surface that whole week, in the tolerance he had shown both of them, even after the unfortunate accidents.

Accidents caused because Harriet wanted so badly to do everything right, was so nervous around him, so afraid she would say exactly the wrong thing, do exactly the wrong thing. She had wanted him to see her as grown-up and mature.

So of course he had seen her as a kid.

And of course she had spent the entire week doing things wrong, clumsily, self-consciously aware of the newfound feeling inside her.

She would have absolutely died if he'd thought of her as pretty back then.

Because she had fallen in love with him within minutes. Maybe even seconds.

She knew it to be ridiculous now. From the perspective

of a woman who had had four years to think about it, to travel the world, to experience many adventures, to marry badly, she knew how ridiculous her younger and more naive self had been.

When she had seen the results of the vote conducted at the Sunny Peak Mall she had known how ridiculous her twenty-two-year-old self had been.

Ridiculous, but not alone.

Women loved him, pure and simple.

She had been given the rarest of things—a second chance. To prove she could be competent, that she was not in the least clumsy or accident prone.

And she had a second chance for him to see her as attractive, the thick bottle-bottom glasses no longer a necessity because of the miracle of laser surgery.

Her teeth as straight and white as money and time and steel could make them.

She knew how to dress now in a way that made her height and slenderness an asset. He might not like the skirt, but she hadn't missed how his eyes had touched on the length of her legs. Her tendency to freckle was becoming less with each year, revealing a startling, lovely complexion underneath. She had learned how to use makeup to show off her eyes and her cheekbones. Some days, like today, she could almost tame the wild mop of her hair.

But most of all she had been give a second chance to prove she was not in love with him.

Not even close. She had been a gauche and unworldly young woman the first time she had met Tyler Jordan. Male influences had been somewhat lacking in her life, as her mother had been a single parent. She had one sister. Despite her height, or maybe because of it, Harriet had always been invisible to the boys in high school and then, disappointingly, in college.

No wonder she had been so completely bowled over by Ty Jordan. In his form-hugging jeans, with those arm muscles rippling, his straight teeth flashing, he'd exuded a male potency, completely without thought on his part, against which she had been defenseless. Even his silences, to her, had seemed to be charged with some male magic that was both foreign and exciting.

But she was not a naive young girl anymore, and she had a secret agenda here. To take back a heart she had given when she hadn't known better. To take back her power.

A deep, muffled woof reminded her of the surprise she had for him. Not a good start in proving herself, but not her fault.

"Stacey asked me to bring Basil out. Her landlord is on to him, and she's going to get evicted."

"Basil?" Tyler was peering over her shoulder. She glanced back. The dog had his big nose pressed mournfully against the window of her small car and was looking at them with pleading, red-rimmed eyes.

"The Saint Bernard?" he asked, incredulous. "My sister sent me the Saint Bernard that knows how to open a fridge? I don't believe this."

"Don't shoot the messenger," she said, leaning in carefully and hooking up the leash. The interior of her car had a slightly raunchy odor to it, which she could only hope was not also clinging to her.

"Don't tempt me," he said sourly.

Should she just tell him who she was? But then he would be expecting the worst from her from the very beginning. How could it be a real second chance if he had preconceived notions? If he thought of her as the Harriet who blushed every time she spoke and choked on her food at dinner because he even made her self-conscious about chewing?

The dog barreled out of the car as soon as she flipped the seat forward, loped to the end of its lead, reared up and placed its saucer-size paws on Tyler's chest and licked his face.

She wondered if Basil was female. The man was irresistible.

Except Harrie planned to resist him. This time everything was going according to her plan. She was a professional photographer. She'd been in war zones. She'd traveled the world. She knew how to stay calm while under fire.

Under fire. How about on fire?

She'd worked with some of the world's most attractive men and made the mistake of marrying one of them. She should be immune to their charms.

And she was!

But much of Ty Jordan's charm was in the fact he was unaware he possessed it. If he had any idea that he was infinitely appealing, he shrugged it off as unimportant, not an asset that helped him produce cattle or run a ranch or raise a younger sister.

And he was more than good-looking. Eighteen hundred women had seen that right away, and placed their one precious checkmark, their vote for the perfect calendar guy, beside his name and picture.

He was tall, at least two inches taller than Harriet's embarrassing five foot ten. His shoulders were enormous and mirrored the strength that had allowed him to stand firm even when the beluga-size dog launched itself at him.

And his shoulders weren't enormous because of four days a week power lifting at the gym, either.

They were enormous from throwing bales and breaking green colts and wrestling cattle.

"Get down," he ordered the dog, and backed up the firmness of the command by removing the paws from his chest and shoving on the dog's huge head. With the other arm he swiped his face where the dog had slurped on him.

The simple movement made the sun gleam off the dark hairs on arms that rippled with sinewy muscle. Harrie noticed how the short sleeves of the T-shirt stretched over the bulge of his biceps, molding them. His arms were sun browned, even this early in the year, and his forearms were corded with muscle, his wrists big and square.

The shirt, decorated now with two large paw prints and a splotch of drool, hugged the mounds of deep pectoral muscles, then tapered over broad, hard ribs to a flat waist. The T-shirt was tucked into faded jeans, belted with a scarred brown leather belt. The buckle was worn casually, but it winked solid silver, and Harriet saw it depicted a horse, head down and back arched, trying to get rid of a rider.

Black lettering proclaimed: Wind River Saddle Bronc Champion.

It suddenly occurred to her that her interest in the buckle had put her eyes in the wrong vicinity for too long.

She looked up swiftly.

He had folded his arms over his chest and was looking at her sardonically.

"Do you ride broncs?" she asked, just to let him know she had read the buckle in its entirety.

"No," he replied curtly.

"That's too bad," she said, flashing him what she hoped was a professionally indifferent smile. "It would have made a great photograph."

He narrowed his eyes. "Get this straight right now. We

are not organizing my life for your photo ops. You're going to follow me around, snap a few pictures, and go home.''

She was thinking of the belt buckle. Stacey had told her he went to rodeos before his parents had died, leaving him with Stacey. Before a boy had to become a man. Facts, she reminded herself, that she was not supposed to know.

And yet facts that would help her capture the essence of him on film, an essence he seemed particularly eager not to reveal as he stood there glowering at her.

But it was the essence of him that made him so teeth-grindingly sexy.

She reminded herself she was a photographer now. Not a starstruck kid. He wanted her to be intimidated by him and she could not allow herself that luxury. She was entitled to look at his face. To study it. To know it.

And so she did.

He had dark hair, the midnight black of a summer sky just before the storm. His hair was close-cropped, sticking up a touch in the front. His face was perfection, and she knew, because she had photographed the faces of some of the world's most perfect men. Or men who were considered perfect in the looks department, anyway.

She looked at his face and tried to dissect the appeal of it. It had strong lines, particularly the line from his jawbone to his chin. His chin was square, the cleft so faint it could almost be overlooked. A good photograph would show it, though.

His cheekbones were high, and the hollow from the edge of his mouth to the line of his jaw was pronounced. His lips were full and firm and were bracketed by faint lines, stern and down turned. His nose was strong and straight. The faint white ridge of a scar at the bridge of it only underscored his rugged masculine appeal.

But she knew, finally, it was his eyes that took him over the edge, from a nice-looking guy to something beyond. His eyes were almond shaped, fringed with a spiky abundance of black lash. The eyes themselves were the dark rich brown of melted chocolate, but it was the look in them that defined him.

Unflinching. Steady. Calm. Strong. Deep.

And yet some mystery resided there, too. It was not exactly wariness, but a certain aloofness. His eyes told his story: that he was a man who chose to walk alone, who knew his own strength completely and relied on it without thought or hesitation.

A lot to know perhaps from one glance at a man.

Except she had had so much more than that. A week that shone in her memory, a few photographs she had taken that had become worn over the years from handling.

A memory of the way those eyes changed when the laughter sparked deep in their depths.

The dog caught a movement out of the corner of his eye and flung his great head, drool flying as he did so. Harrie leaped back to avoid her suit being splattered by dog spit.

It was a nice suit. Extremely professional, gray silk, tight enough to be feminine. She had worn it to travel in, with flat-heeled loafers.

Okay, the skirt was a little shorter than it should have been, and she could have done up one more blouse button, and it would have made more sense to show up in slacks, but still—

The dog let out a sudden deep bay. She was completely unprepared for the power of the beast as he leaped to his feet and charged toward a cow and calf that had come out from behind a shelter and were now nosing the new spring grass in the pasture adjoining the driveway.

Harrie felt her shoulder jerk and the leash burn through her hand. She caught the loop of the leash at the end of it and held on for dear life.

Stacey had told her, laughing, after their visit to the ranch, *Ty was amazed you didn't stampede the cattle.*

Playfully he had called her Lady Disaster. She was not going to have this stupid dog stampede the cattle within minutes of her arriving this time—this time when everything was going to be so different.

Off balance, as the powerful dog charged toward the cattle pen, baying with excitement, she lost her footing and fell forward. Undeterred, but slowed down, the huge animal continued forward grinding her knees and face, not to mention her beautiful silk suit, into the dirt and grass.

Ty leaped, grabbed the lead, planted his heels and jerked back hard.

The dog came to an instant halt, glanced back and hung his head remorsefully.

"Are you all right?" Ty asked with irritation, rather than compassion. He was at her elbow now, yanking her to her feet.

"I'm fine," she snapped, jerking her arm away from him, looking down at her ruined suit.

"You're hurt."

He was crouched down in front of her, but nothing prepared her for the touch of his hand on her knee. A knee now devoid of nylon.

He looked up at her.

And she sighed. This was an omen. Five minutes in his presence, and catastrophe had already struck. Never mind that she had him exactly where she wanted him—on bended knee.

It was for the wrong reasons. He was looking at her knee with about the same expression she was sure he would use on an injured cow. Detached. Competent.

"I'm fine," she said tersely. "It's a scratch. I have a Band-Aid in my bag."

"The problem with a cut out here," he said, putting his hands on his knees and rising to his feet, giving the dog a quick jerk on the lead to let him know he was still there, "is that we have a lot of livestock around. We can have all kinds of nasty little things wriggling around in the soil. I'll have to put antiseptic on it."

No. No. No.

This was not how she had planned things. At all. "It's fine," she said.

"Humor me." Still controlling the dog, he opened the passenger side of her car and settled the straps of her carry bag over one shoulder, the strap of her huge camera bag over the other.

"I can take that," she said.

He stepped away from her easily. "I'll get it." It was said with a certain firmness that set her teeth on edge. How had Stacey become so independent in the presence of such old-fashioned male arrogance? Maybe Stacey rebelled against his arrogance. Her boyfriend appeared to be Ty's polar opposite: long-haired, liberal, artistic, sweet-tempered.

He led the way up to the house, giving the dog's leash a snap every time it lunged forward.

The walk gave Harriet an unfortunate view of the back of him. Broad back, a certain angry stiffness in the set of his shoulders, his fanny gorgeous nonetheless in those faded jeans, his legs long and lean and strong. By the time they arrived at the back door, she felt as if she was practically panting, and not entirely because of the length of Ty's powerful stride.

The dog was walking quietly at his side, sending him upward glances as though longing for his approval.

"I was going to put you in the bunkhouse," he said, opening the door and standing back from it. "But I can see that won't work. Cringle said you'd be here a week. Would you say that's a fair estimate?"

"I don't mind the bunkhouse," she said tersely. "A week maximum. If everything goes right."

Why did she feel so unsure of that, suddenly? Everything on her photo shoots always went right. Because of her news photography background she had become adept at getting wonderful pictures without great lighting, without a huge team, without makeup artists.

She could just imagine what Ty Jordan would have to say about a makeup artist.

"And the guys surely wouldn't mind you sharing the bunkhouse, either, but you can have my little sister's room." This was said with the quiet authority of a man who didn't expect to be questioned.

She was sorely tempted to insist on the bunkhouse. She could tell him she had bunked with guys before. That war zones had a way of blurring lines and stripping modesty. But something about the tiny chink in his armor when he said "little sister" stopped her.

This was the side of him she wanted to capture on camera. The personal side. And she would have far more chance of doing that if she was camped out under the same roof as him.

He tied the dog to the outside of the door handle before he followed her into the house.

"Bathroom's through here," he said, dropping her bag

on the floor. "If you want to slip off those things, I'll get the first-aid kit."

She said thank-you when what she really wanted to say was "go to hell." She retrieved her bag, went into the bathroom and closed the door. She took off the ruined pantyhose, looked down at the ragged scrape across her knee.

She'd been a war correspondent for two years with nary a scratch.

She looked in the mirror. Her suit was ruined. Her face was smudged. Her hair was standing on end. She took off the suit and opened her suitcase. The all-important first impression had been made. Hopefully the first thirty seconds of it had more impact than the second thirty, but she doubted it. She put on a pair of jeans and a T-shirt. If she was taking her power back, she certainly wasn't going to fix her hair, or refresh her make-up for him.

She did remove the smudge from her face before marching back out of the bathroom.

When she came out he was in the kitchen, rummaging through a white metal box with a red cross on the side of it. He didn't even glance up at her.

The kitchen was unchanged, she thought looking around. Plain, a utilitarian room that served a function.

But it held memories, too—her and Stacey making a mess creating homemade pizza, him coming in, dirty from work, sexy as sin, and giving them hell. Then he'd softened the blow by saying how good it smelled, and he couldn't wait to try it. She remembered playing cards at that scarred kitchen table with Stacey. He'd been tired, physical weariness bowing his shoulders, but when Stacey had pleaded, he had joined them, reluctantly, and ended up showing them how to play poker. Losing his reluctance a little later, he'd showed them a game called Blind Baseball.

She could not remember the rules or the point of the game, only that they had held the cards up on their foreheads where the other players could see them but they couldn't see their own.

She could remember the laughter that had filled that room, that had chased that faint weariness from his face. His laughter had made him seem younger and more human. Incredibly, it had made him even more handsome than he had seemed before, and that had been plenty handsome. The moment had shone with a light almost iridescent, had stolen her breath from her lungs, and the joy of other good moments in her life had paled before the perfection of that one.

"Are you all right?"

He was looking at her closely.

"Yes," she said. "I told you it was just a scratch."

But she knew what a scratch could do. Four years ago he had scratched the surface of an uninitiated heart.

And that scratch had festered and grown to a wound.

"Have a seat over here, Miss Snow."

"Call me Harrie."

"I don't think so."

"Pardon?" She sat down at the chair he'd pulled out for her.

"I just can't look at you and call you Harry." He knelt down in front of her, completely unselfconscious, the medical kit on the ground beside him. He rolled up the leg of her jeans, without apparently noticing she had changed outfits. She found herself holding the side of the chair as if she was getting ready for takeoff.

"Fine by me, Mr. Jordan. Do you think you could make that Ms. Snow?"

He shrugged, indifferent, and didn't invite her to call
him Tyler, or Ty, as she had called him last time she was
here. Looking at the top of his head, his dark hair shiny
as silk, she wondered if there was any of that laughter-
filled boy left in him.

"I'm not going to hurt you," he said, his eyes flicking
over the white of her knuckles on the edge of her chair.

"Thank you. I know." He hadn't even touched her yet,
for God's sake.

The touch, when it came, was everything she had
feared, everything she had braced herself for.

It was strong, infinitely competent, as he carefully
cleaned the area around the scrape on her knee. The skin
of his palm brushed her lower knee as he swabbed her
cut, and it was leather tough, the hand of man who worked
outdoors in extreme weather and handled shovels and
reins and newborn calves. The hand of a man who drove
big trucks and chopped wood and fixed fences.

And yet there was none of that toughness in his touch.
He was careful and extremely gentle, a man, she reminded
herself, who had looked after scraped knees before. And
broken arms.

"There, I think I've got the grit out," he said, inspect-
ing it carefully. His breath whispered across the dampness
of the skin surrounding her scrape, and she had to close
her eyes against the sensation that tingled through her
tummy, the insane desire to lean forward and ask him to
kiss it better.

He dabbed iodine on with a cotton swab on a wand that
came out of the bottle. Thankfully the application required
no direct contact, and allowed her to marshal her defenses.

But then he carefully cut a square of gauze, held that
over the scrape, the warmth of his hand encircling her
kneecap. With his other hand he juggled the medical tape,

cutting off pieces, then pressing them firmly into place, his fingertips trailing liquid fire down skin she had not really been aware was so sensitive until now.

"All done," he announced, and Harrie wasn't sure if she was safe or sorry. He rolled her pant leg down and got to his feet.

It was about the sexiest thing that had ever happened to her, which probably summed up her pathetic luck with the opposite sex, including her ex-husband, quite nicely.

"Thank you," she said, and clambered to her feet, wiped her sweaty palms on her jeans. "I'm fine. That was completely unnecessary. Nice. But unnecessary."

She could feel herself getting red. Why had she said *nice?* "I meant kind," she stammered, "not nice."

She could tell he found her making the distinction amusing. Harrie could feel herself becoming exactly the same bumpkin she had been four years ago. She had to get this situation under control.

"I was just looking out for myself, Ms. Snow. I'm not real anxious to have you getting sick on the place. I don't want to be doing any baby-sitting."

It had been about him. She had the sudden feeling that coming back here had not been a great idea after all. He was going out of his way to make himself unlikable.

"Well, then let's get to work, Mr. Jordan. As you know, my challenge will be to create the illusion of four seasons over the next week. I was hoping we could use the fireplace for the December shot. Hang a few stockings."

"How do you know I have a fireplace?" he asked.

She should have known this would happen sometime. That she would let it slip that she was more familiar with him and this house than she should be.

"Your sister told me," she lied brightly. "We tossed

around the idea of how to create the seasons a little bit at the office.''

Wasn't that just the problem with little white lies? She saw the faintest flicker in his eyes. He didn't like that he had been discussed at the office.

Harriet had always been an absolutely terrible liar, and she could see by the long look he gave her she had not improved in that department. ''I'll just follow you around with the camera,'' she said brightly. ''Whatever you normally do, go ahead and do it. You won't even know I'm there.''

''I usually have a shower right now,'' he drawled, watching her.

She stared at him and gulped. She could feel a horrible wave of heat moving up her neck to her face.

''In the middle of the day?'' she managed to challenge him, her voice a squeak.

''Just making sure your limits are the same as mine,'' he said. ''I'm a private man, Ms. Snow. I'll let you know when it's okay to take pictures.''

She begged herself to challenge him, to not let him back her down. She lifted her chin and said, ''I don't know, Mr. Jordan, a nice steamy shower shot would probably sell a whole pile of calendars.''

Then she spoiled the effect entirely by blushing. She gulped and looked at her feet.

She saw his booted feet move into her range of vision. She refused to look up, and then she felt that hand, so familiar to her after the knee episode, touch her chin ever so lightly.

She lifted her face to him and didn't look away when he scanned her quizzically.

''Don't play with fire, Ms. Snow.''

What could be more embarrassing than a full-grown

mature woman being embarrassed by something so innocuous?

Something changed in his eyes. A puzzled look came into them.

She was almost sure he recognized her, or if he didn't, something had tickled his memory, troubled him.

"They should have sent the man," he said.

She bristled. "I happen to be very good at my job. And for your information, I've been a war correspondent. I've lived in close quarters with men in very rough conditions."

"Really?" he said, his eyes narrowed as if he didn't believe a word of it.

"Really," she said coolly. "Besides, women get better shots of men, for obvious reasons."

"I don't find them obvious. Could you explain?"

"It's the male preening thing. 'Little lady, let me show you how big and strong I am.'"

He stared at her, and a muscle jumped in his jaw. He gave his head a shake. "Is there any chance we could have you out of here in less than a week?"

"Cooperating would help."

"Can you ride a horse?"

Now this was the question she'd been dreading. She'd fallen off a horse last time she'd been here. It had been the first time she had ever ridden, and it hadn't been the horse's fault at all.

Ty had been riding in the lead, Stacey behind him.

And Harrie, last in line, had been leaning way too far out, mesmerized by the way he looked in the saddle, her first cheap 35 mm raised to her eye, wanting that photograph so badly.

She'd fallen and broken her arm, ending her visit.

The humiliation had led her to take riding lessons the

following year while on assignment in England. She had never really got the feel for it. She could manage walk, trot, canter, stop, but the instructor had told her what she already knew.

She repeated it to him. "I can manage the basics, but I don't have a good seat."

She saw his eyes flick to the area in question, and she saw the comeback flash through his eyes, knew she had left herself wide open to it.

But apparently he had decided making her blush was not that amusing, because he said nothing for a moment. He was still watching her, puzzled, and she had a feeling he was a breath away from figuring that puzzle out when a loud noise ripped through the house, a banshee wail of nails being pulled from wood, of hinges parting. The noise was followed by a crash and a splinter.

Ty raced to the kitchen window, and she followed.

Basil was racing across the yard, straight toward the cattle pen that had intrigued him before. Ty's back door, still attached to the leash, skidded along behind him.

Ty said three words in a row that would have made a sailor blush, then hurtled toward the door. She picked up her camera, but had to stop and put her shoes on. Then she went in hot pursuit. This was more like it. The war zone she could handle.

Chapter Three

If there was a feeling that Ty Jordan hated more than any other in the world it was this one: he did not like being out of control. He was aware of that dislike bubbling away briskly inside of him as he bolted after the dog.

A dog *she* had brought with her.

The she who should have been a *he*.

Male preening. As if he was some peacock put here for her entertainment.

She had better figure this out real quick: the Bar ZZ was Ty Jordan's property, his domain, and he had already decided he wasn't rearranging anything about his lifestyle to accommodate the stupid calendar.

He had been made a promise—by Cringle himself and by his sister—that his life would not be disturbed or disrupted in any way.

That blinking dog was heading right for the cow and calf pen. With a burst of speed Ty caught up to the door that was twisting and turning and flopping on the lead behind the dog. He threw himself on top of it, hoping at least to slow the dog down.

Ms. Snow, whom he could not think of as Harry, even in his mind, yelled something at him, but he didn't quite catch what it was.

Two hundred and three pounds landing on the door did slow the dog down—minutely. Ty was now bouncing along behind the dog, riding the door on his stomach, like a surfer on a board. He found the door handle and unraveled the leash where it was tied to it.

"Watch your face," she yelled, and he realized that was what she had yelled the first time.

He cast her one brief scornful look before he managed to unknot the leash from the door handle. He pulled it free, rolled from the door, got to his feet and hauled in Basil, who came to him happily, his big tongue lolling out of his mouth, his tail flagging.

"Kiss me and your days are numbered," he warned.

"I beg your pardon?"

"I wasn't talking to you." He bent over at the waist, breathing hard. He became aware of the click and whir of a camera, straightened and glared at her.

She lowered the camera, studied him and then nodded, satisfied. "I was worried about your face," she said. "A black eye or a bruise could make things complicated."

"Oh, like things aren't complicated enough," he returned, insulted to be evaluated like a piece of merchandise. At least he had an out he registered in the back of his mind. If she bugged him enough, he'd go try and break that renegade horse. That should be good for a few battle scars on his all-important face.

Of course, he'd have to do it in the dead of night or his humiliation might be plastered on calendars for all the world to see.

It's one week, he told himself. Twelve usable photos. He could do that. He'd made a promise.

Never mind that it had been in a moment of weakness.

And in fairness, though he didn't particularly feel he wanted to be fair, it wasn't her fault Stacey had saddled her with the dog.

And it wasn't her fault that she was beautiful. When she had gotten out of her car, he had been watching from the shadow of the barn. Watching as she stretched, pressing her slender curves into the flimsy fabric of that outfit, watching as she gave her hair a shake, ran her fingers through red curls that caught the sun and wove it into flame.

He'd thought she must be lost and had emerged from the barn to point her in the right direction. But a glance at his watch had given him the ugly feeling she was probably the photographer from Francis Cringle.

The first thing he'd noticed as he got closer hadn't been her height. That had registered only peripherally.

He had noticed her eyes. Brown, shot through with green and gold, sparkling with light that looked as if it could only mean trouble to a confirmed bachelor like himself.

And then he had noticed her smile, tentative, almost shy, not in keeping with the polished air she carried.

It had made him so mad he wanted to spit—not the polish, but that hint of vulnerability. It meant he couldn't be nearly as mean as he wanted to be.

He didn't have time for women. He'd been down that road two or three times before he'd wised up the last time. He'd missed the part of his life, plain and simple, when a man learned how to court a woman.

When he might have been dating, planning his own

future, he'd been raising a little girl instead. Running a ranch.

He never had anything left over to give to a relationship. And it seemed to him relationships demanded a lot. Time. Effort. Commitment. He had nothing left over when a day was done.

And once Stacey was gone and that might have changed, he was set in his ways. He didn't know how to meet people, and besides he didn't want to go to movies and hold hands. He didn't want to sit across candlelit tables trying to think of things to say. He didn't want to have to think of things like buying flowers.

It was enough of a nuisance having to lay in groceries.

Stacey who had become an annoying expert on romance the more involved she got with her hippie, said there was no romance in him. But she said it as if it was a bad thing.

What was so bad about a man working so hard that he fell into bed at night exhausted, his sleep deep and untroubled, his world a place where he knew exactly what was going to happen next?

So, Ty Jordan resented that his *guest* had been here less than an hour, and he had already felt the hard ache of hunger. He wished he had let her get the Band-Aid out of her bag after all. Then he would never have had any reason to be touching the silky slenderness of Ms. Snow's leg. Her kneecap had struck him as a foolishly fragile thing, about the size of a silver dollar.

But then women were foolishly fragile things, not cut out for this kind of life, this kind of loneliness. Not unless they were raised in it, and the women he knew like that, who he'd gone to school with and grown up with, had long ago been snapped up. Snapped up at dances and drive-ins and neighborhood barbecues, events he had been too busy or too tired to attend.

It wasn't Ms. Snow's fault he'd chosen to live like a hermit, away from temptations that complicated a man's life, complications that could wrest it from his control.

The truth was, he liked control better than just about anything else. If someone had asked him, Ty Jordan, if he wanted a brand-new fire-red Ferrari or if he wanted tomorrow to unfold the very same as today, he would have picked what he already had.

A life of working outdoors with animals, the freedom of never having called another man his boss, the sight of cattle grazing in the shadow of mountains that greeted him out his window when he woke up at five every morning.

So, it had annoyed him that he'd had a pretty masculine reaction to touching her kneecap and had thought he would just test the limits of his control—and hers—with that remark about the shower.

Her face had gotten so red he'd thought he was going to have to get the fire extinguisher.

He'd be alone too long, that was the problem. Stacey was absolutely right about him. He was cranky and a control freak, and there was little hope of him ever changing now.

She was a beautiful woman; he was a man. Human, after all.

But if he was going to get out of this week with his world still soundly in his control, that acknowledgment was going to be the end of it.

And he planned to have complete control, dog and female photographer notwithstanding. Ignoring her as best he could with that camera clicking away, he dragged the dog back up to the yard and tied it to the thick yard-light post. He'd tied horses there before. If they couldn't take it down, he doubted that the dog could.

He turned to her. "I have to go check cattle. I'm riding to do it. Can you hold your own? Because I don't have time to baby-sit."

"I can hold my own," she said defiantly, and then as a little afterthought, "as long as the horse is not too lively."

"Oh, that would be Blackie, all right. She used to buck on the circuit. Black Death is her registered name."

She blanched, and he found the decency in himself to mutter, "I'm kidding."

"Oh. Oh, good."

He strode down to the barn, aware of how her long legs kept pace with his, and caught his saddle horse, Mikey. She took a picture. He threw her a halter, hoping to distract her from her mission to immortalize him on film. "That one," he said pointing to the sway-backed old mare munching contentedly.

He watched her closely. She was determined not to show she was nervous. But he knew when people were nervous around horses. It was that tiny step back, instead of forward, the almost imperceptible hesitation, the soft, crooning talk with just a little catch at the edge of the words.

Still, she knew how to put a halter on, which was more than he'd expected. And Blackie was a good baby-sitter, patient and forgiving, neither of which quality he could claim for himself.

He led the way into the barn and gestured for her to lead the horse into the first open stall. He watched with a critical eye as she did a perfect schoolgirl knot with the lead shank and asked for the grooming equipment.

Lessons. He'd be willing to bet she'd had lessons. He

left her to it and brought his horse into the stall next to hers, where he could keep an eye on her over the four-foot divider between stalls. When Blackie was falling asleep under her vigorous brushing, he turned his back on her and tried his best not to think about how she looked.

He had almost succeeded in thinking his own thoughts when the flash went off in his eyes. His horse jumped sideways but thankfully had enough respect for him that it went away from him, instead of crushing him up against the stall wall. Mikey turned and looked at her, white-eyed.

"Sorry," she said, aghast, her long legs straddling the half wall of the stall.

"I thought I asked you to tell me when you were going to do that."

"But I want spontaneous pictures."

"Of a dead man?"

"I said sorry. And you can't be dead. You're still talking."

He had to turn away from her quickly, before she saw the little smile that tickled his lips entirely against his will. But he stripped the smile from his voice when he said, "Look, a greenhorn can be the most dangerous thing on a ranch. Let me know if you're going to use the flash."

"Aye, aye, sir."

There was a touch of sardonic humor in her own voice, and something inside him felt a strange little twinge. Of what? He'd felt it once already with her. When she had talked about her seat on the horse and she had blushed defensively, stealing the comeback from his lips and filling him with this same feeling.

He tried to pinpoint it and failed. Recognition seemed to come close, but men didn't forget when they met a woman who looked like this.

"How about if instead of spooking the horses, you just

get ready?'' Get off the wall, and get her long legs out of his eye level.

"Aye, aye, sir," she said again.

He was finished well before her, and looked over the divider into her stall to see how she was doing. The lessons were written all over her careful approach to grooming. He watched as she took her own hanky out of her pocket, and cleaned the dust out of Blackie's nose, much to Blackie's horrified amazement.

He brought a saddle out, tossed it on the stall divider. "Can you handle that?"

"Of course," she said with supreme confidence, but the glance she leveled at the saddle showed her doubt. He stuck around. He let her struggle with the saddle for longer than a gentleman would have, before he moved into the stall with her.

It had never struck him before that the stalls were too narrow, but he knew now they were. There was no room to move, to maneuver away from her, the soft scent that wafted from her, the soft heat where his shoulder was nearly touching her arm.

Clenching his jaw, he showed her the cinch knot and then undid it and watched while she did it herself.

The aroma of her seemed to intensify, mingling with the barn smells and the scent of Blackie. It tickled his nose, soft and feminine.

He tried to place her aroma and decided it was like the honeysuckle that grew wild at the edge of the porch, only way more subtle and far more sensuous.

It was in defense against that aroma that his voice sounded so stern, razor edged, the kind of tone a drill sergeant took to a buck private. "It's not tight enough. Do it again."

Ignoring the growing frustration in her eyes, he made

her redo the cinch half a dozen times. Well, let her be mad. It was for her own good. He had to be completely satisfied the saddle wouldn't tip over if her balance was bad, and if he didn't have the patience to be diplomatic about it, so what? He was a cowboy, not a kindergarten teacher. His profession rarely required diplomacy.

He told himself it was for her safety, but when he saw the blistering anger in her eyes after the sixth time, he knew the truth. It was for his own safety. He wanted her to keep her distance. A man could only stand so much of that honeysuckle-at-night smell before he threw his absolute need for control to the wind and decided to take some chances with life.

He showed her how to slip the bridle on, then took it out and made her do that herself, too.

Blackie, like any horse worth its salt, could smell a greenhorn and gave Ms. Snow a run for her money before accepting the bit. Ty refused to help, watched with his arms folded firmly over his chest as she tried to snag the artfully dodging head.

To her credit, Ms. Snow didn't give up and didn't look to him for help.

They walked the horses outside and tied them to a hitching post. He showed her how to check the feet. By the time they were done that, little sweat smears were appearing under her arms, which made her smell better than ever. She also had a little smudge of dirt across one cheek, and her hair was taking on a decidedly unruly look.

Not the polished woman who had gotten out of her car a little while ago.

The long legs should have made it easy for her to mount Blackie, who was on the smallish side, but her jeans were too new and didn't bend easily at the knee. Or maybe it was her knee that didn't bend all that easily after her injury.

Whatever the reason, that was one place he wasn't helping her out.

His hand on her fanny would blow his whole world apart. So he watched as she struggled into the saddle, took up the reins, one in each hand, English style, and then realized her lead shank was still firmly attached to the hitching post.

For the very first time, she gave him a look that was faintly pleading, and he could tell it cost her.

Just like it cost him to ignore it. But his mother had always said, *Ty, start as you mean to go,* and he had no intention of being her manservant over the next week. He spent a lot of time on and off horses during a day. He needed to be satisfied, right now, that she could pull her own weight.

If she couldn't, it would be a good enough excuse to send her packing.

She dismounted and unlatched the lead rope then clambered back into the saddle. She actually moaned out loud when she saw her camera stuff still sitting on the ground, but by the third time she got on that horse she was getting better at it.

He knew how to leap on a horse from the back, the way they did it in movies, hands on the rump leapfrogging up into the saddle. It appalled him that it even occurred to him to do it. Male preening.

He very deliberately put his foot in the stirrup and got on slowly, with as little show as he could manage.

"Can I use my flash?"

"We're outside."

"It's fill-in flash," she said, as if he would understand what that meant. He nodded sagely, just as if he did. He wondered, uneasily, if that was a variation on male preening?

He left his rein loose. Maybe Mikey would take exception to it and put him on the ground, on his face, hopefully.

That would be the end of Ms. Snow and his disturbing discovery about himself and male preening.

But Mikey stood placidly for having his picture taken.

"Don't ask me to smile," Ty said.

"Don't worry. The pictures are supposed to look natural."

He frowned at her, not certain why he felt so annoyed that she was buying the exact image that he was portraying. She placidly snapped a picture of his scowl, and he turned Mikey away from her and rode out of the yard, leaving her frantically scrambling to put her stuff away. After a while he heard Blackie plodding along behind him. He didn't look back.

"Don't ranchers use four-wheelers, now, and motorcycles?" she asked, when they stopped at the first gate.

He glanced at her. She was already feeling it. He caught her rubbing the inside of her knee.

"Some do," he said, leading his horse through, beckoning for her to follow and closing the gate behind them.

The gate was a post-and-wire affair that hitched by being forced through a loop. It took quite a push to fasten it, and he heard the camera click as he wrestled with it. He couldn't imagine what she found interesting about this particular activity. He looked at her from under the shadow of his cowboy hat.

The camera was to her eye, focused on his arm.

He glanced at the rigid line of the taut muscle in his arm. He had expected he was going to hate this experience; he just hadn't figured on how much. Because a traitorous part of him wanted to flex even more. Just like she had said. *Little lady, let me show you how big and strong I am.* He slammed the gate into place, and with his face carefully blank, he got back on his horse, resisting the temptation to take the horn and swing on without using the stirrup at all.

"But you don't?" she said. "Use motorized vehicles?"

"Nope."

"Why?"

"You'll see in a bit. Are you taking pictures or writing a book?" He glanced back at her and realized she was only trying to be polite and make conversation.

He didn't want to talk to her. He was still reeling from how accurate her perception had been about men. Who knew what he might start talking about given the close proximity of a sympathetic feminine ear?

The loneliness of long winter nights crept into his mind. He banished the thought, working his horse off his leg to occupy his rebellious mind.

The horse was side passing nicely, and of course she was too much of a greenhorn to know he didn't usually ride weaving sideways lines. Soon he spotted the herd of cows and calves on the other side of a swell of land. They had been riding for about twenty minutes now.

"See?" he said. "This is why I don't like using a motorized vehicle."

He pointed, and watched her face when she realized a calf was lying down in the grass nearly right in front of them.

A light came on when she saw the calf, and she looked radiant.

"Oh," she breathed, "he's beautiful."

Well, he couldn't disagree with that, though watching her face light up like that, the feeling came again....

A déjà vu feeling of knowing her when, of course, he knew he did not.

They rode through the herd, and he did a slow check on what cows had calved since he had been here this morning, which ones looked ready. He looked for trouble and was thankful when he saw none.

But when he looked at her face he knew trouble came in lots of different sizes and shapes, and trouble had landed right on his front doorstep, big-time.

He considered loping all the way home. The good thing was it would keep her quiet. The bad thing was it could probably be misconstrued as male preening.

He pointed his horse for home and walked slowly, listening to the click of the camera behind him. He glanced back at her, thinking no one was going to find pictures of his back interesting. What kind of photographer was she?

She was not even looking at him, her camera focused on a newborn calf and then on the smoky shadows of the mountains as the light began to change on them.

He looked a little longer than he should have. Long enough to see the pure wonder in her face, the contented rise and fall of her breath as she drew in a deep gulp of the clean air.

He looked at her just long enough to know that a week was about to become the longest unit of time known to man.

Three days later Ty Jordan knew he had never had a more accurate thought. She was beautiful. But what made her hard to remain cold to was her sense of wonder. She took childish delight in things he took totally for granted. And she did have a sense of fun. The woman made him laugh, even if he tried to hide it. She was energetic and quick-witted, and the more he liked her, the more he pretended not to.

Now it was the third night with her under the same roof. He lay in bed, listening to her rustlings on the other side of the wall. Ty acknowledged that his days of rolling into bed and going instantly to sleep were over.

He wanted to blame the dog, tied outside and barking indignantly. Basil was not, apparently, accustomed to being left outside, and after three nights he was showing no sign of giving in to the idea. The mutt was probably furious about not having free access to the fridge. He also did not understand the words "shut up."

Ty glanced at his bedside clock, then pulled a pillow over his head.

One o'clock in the morning.

The pillow did not blot out the dog's barking in the least. Nor did it blot out the real problem.

In the bedroom right next to his was a long-legged beauty with flaming red hair and gorgeous brown eyes and a figure that made his mouth go dry.

A woman who should have been worldly. After all, she had agreed to stay under the same roof with a man she didn't know.

But who wasn't worldly at all.

The dog stopped barking. Ty held his breath. Maybe Basil had gone to sleep. Harry seemed to him to be a name that would suit the dog. But her?

The name was ugly, and she was beautiful. The name was masculine and she was feminine. He bet it wasn't her real name.

Some gimmick she'd picked up in war zones.

When she'd first told him that, he'd thought he was going to laugh. Her in a war zone? Everything about her seemed soft. No toughness.

But then he'd seen her go to work with her camera. She had an unbelievable intensity of focus. Not the least bit worried about getting dirty, she'd gotten right down in the dirt to get the shots she wanted.

The camera whirred and clicked constantly. He might have even been able to forget it was there, except that she was behind it, changing lenses, changing films, taking light readings, climbing over fences or up into the rafters, or crawling on the ground to get shots she wanted.

Then he'd taken her to the bunkhouse to meet his crew and eat. He had three hands who had been with him for a long, long time and whom Ty thought all women who believed in the romance of the cowboy should have a good hard look at. Pete and Slim were two middle-aged twins, bald and missing teeth and about as handsome as mud. They both chewed tobacco in great revolting gobs, swore as an introduction to each new sentence that they spoke and didn't believe bathing with regularity was either healthy or necessary.

And both of them were worth their weight in gold on this ranch.

So was old Cookie. He couldn't do too much hard work anymore and had turned his energy toward baking in the old woodstove in the bunkhouse. On any given day he experimented with different kinds of bread, cookies, pies and muffins to go with the steaks he grilled every single night. It was still Cookie's wisdom that Ty turned to when he needed advice and good old-fashioned cow sense.

Seeing Ms. Snow with them had made Ty consider possibly she had been in a war zone. She didn't wrinkle her nose at Pete and Slim and she beat Cookie at chess three times every night after dinner.

She won them over by taking countless pictures of their

ugly mugs, and by teasing them with an ease she had not displayed around Ty at all.

He told himself he didn't want to think about her. He really didn't. All he wanted was the blasted dog to give it a rest so he could go to sleep. Had it really been five minutes since he had heard from the dog?

He took the pillow off his head, listened, drew a deep breath.

Then the dog started barking again.

He swore, swung his legs out of bed, pulled on his jeans. He was going to kill Stacey next time he saw her. The dog. The woman. The stupid calendar. All things linked and all Stacey's fault.

Outside his bedroom door, in the pitch-darkness, he collided into her.

They stood in the darkness of the hallway together, too close. He ordered himself to step back, to take his hand off her arm, but he didn't.

"Oh," she whispered, as if she was afraid someone else might be sleeping, "I was going to go do something about the dog. He's making me crazy."

"Me, too." Only, the dog was suddenly squeezed from his mind. What was making him crazy now was the sweet scent of her, the luminousness of her eyes.

Her skin was soft beneath his fingertips.

He let go reluctantly, took a step back. "What were you going to do?"

"Sneak him into my room. What about you?"

He didn't think it would win him any Brownie points to tell her about the twenty-two rifle behind his kitchen door.

Not that he needed Brownie points. "I was going to give him a few bones to gnaw on."

They stood in the hallway, neither of them moving.

"Well, I'll let you go look after him, then," she said.

She was wearing a very short, silky housecoat. He could see the rise and fall of her chest. Her lips were full and shiny, as if she had just licked them. Insanely, he wanted to kiss her.

Or at least the big strong man did.

He leaned toward her, pulled on an invisible string. She leaned toward him. His lips touched hers.

It was heaven and hell, both. Heaven because the taste of her lips was so sweet and tantalizing, just like that honeysuckle she smelled of.

He knew if he bit the tiny base off the flower of a honeysuckle, a teasing taste of the sweetest honey scooted through his mouth, and made him want more.

And that tiny little kiss had done the same thing.

But that was the hell part. There was some innocence in that kiss that he could barely fathom. She was staring at him, her eyes huge. He could see she was trembling. She actually took her fist to her mouth and bit on it, as if to stop the shaking.

The gesture stopped him cold. He stared at her, that feeling back, stronger than ever.

And then his heart sank, and he knew kissing her was out of the question. Someone else had bitten her fist just like that. After the well went dry. After the calves were disappearing in the direction of High River.

"Harriet," he growled. "Harriet Pendleton."

She laughed nervously, and he wondered how he had managed not to know before. The laugh was so familiar.

"All grown up," she said, as if that in some way made what had happened all right. As if in some way that meant they could continue.

Ha. She was a friend of his sister's. She could be eighty in her rocking chair, and that was all he would ever see.

A kid.

Off-limits to him.

The week, even with three days carefully checked off his calendar, suddenly felt as if it was going to be endless, an eternity.

His mission was simplified though: to get through their remaining four days without looking at her lips again. Because those were not the lips of a kid. Actually, hers wasn't the body of a kid, either.

He resented the fact she hadn't told him who she was, so he could have set his mind properly in the first place. Resetting it, after certain thoughts had attached themselves to her, was going to be quite a bit harder.

And now his life was more complex. Before, his battle had been simply not to like her. Now he couldn't even be a little bit mean to her. He said a curse word under his breath and turned on his heel to go look after the dog.

Chapter Four

"**S**hhh, don't bark. I'll get you a cookie."

Harriet listened to the man trying to sneak the dog by her bedroom. She glanced at her bedside clock and groaned. It was five-thirty in the morning.

She came wide awake. Ty was trying to get out of the house without waking her. After what had happened last night, he was probably thinking of saddling a horse and heading for Mexico, like the hero in an old Western.

He wasn't getting away with it! She threw back the bedcovers.

And then, just like that, his efforts to be quiet were over. His voice exploded from downstairs. He said five words in a row that she had never heard, not even in the war zone, and in a tone that would have stripped paint.

She heard the dog whine.

She climbed from bed and yanked on her jeans. She would have liked to have given her choice of clothes this morning careful consideration, but if she was not mistaken, that was the sound of broken glass being cleaned up in the kitchen. She pulled a navy-blue T-shirt from her suitcase, and her quick, casual glance in the mirror told her it was precisely the right choice.

The T-shirt said she was interested in getting the job done, that she was ready and willing and able to crawl through dirt and grass and manure to do that job. The T-shirt said the job was everything and how she looked as a woman was secondary. Not even secondary. Not even a little bit important. She regarded the T-shirt for all of thirty seconds before burying it back in her suitcase and choosing a lovely pale-green sweater that looked profes-sional *and* made her look every inch a woman.

She had expected disaster when she confronted herself in the mirror—bags under her eyes, hair every which way—and so she was surprised at what she saw. She did not look nearly as tired as she felt.

In fact, there was a soft glow about her, a sparkle in her eyes, that made her look rested and, well, ready.

"Ready for what?" she demanded softly of herself.

More kisses, a rebel voice inside her yelled.

"No! Not open for discussion. Not even open for think-ing about!" She resolved she would not say one word about last night to Tyler Jordan and not think one thought about it to herself. It was over. It was done. If she intended to keep her sanity, it was not happening again.

It had hardly even been a kiss, no, a mere brushing of lips. Still, it had served as a reality check. She was going to claim back her power? She was going to prove that Ty had no effect on her? That she had matured beyond all that?

One word formed in her brain: Ha!

She realized she was thinking about it, even though she had resolved absolutely not to. "I will not be a romantic fool,'' she told herself firmly. She took one more look at herself and ran a hand through her hair. And then a brush.

She told herself worrying about one's appearance was not in the same category as being a romantic fool.

Ty was bent over the broom, sweeping glass shards off the floor when she went into the kitchen. The floor swam in milk. Pickles were scattered. A block of cheese, still in its plastic wrapper, had been partially devoured. Basil was lying at the doorway, his eyes sad, his head resting on his paws as he regarded Ty.

''Go back to bed,'' Ty said curtly. ''Sorry I woke you.''

Ha. And let him make his break for Mexico?

''What happened?''

''I took pity on him and brought him in my bedroom last night. Guess what? He knows how to open bedroom doors as well as fridge doors. He appears to have let himself out for a midnight snack.''

She felt a little smile tug on her lips.

''And it isn't funny.''

The little gurgle of laughter slipped out. ''Come on, Ty. It's a little bit funny. Admit it.'' She bent over and began picking pickles out of the puddles on the floor.

''I thought you might want to sleep in,'' Ty said, ''since you were up so late last night.''

''Up so late?''

''It's an old house. The walls are paper thin. I could hear you rustling around until about three in the morning.''

''Which means you must have been awake, too, to hear it.''

''How can a man sleep with all that racket?'' he said defensively, and turned and dumped the dustpan full of glass into the garbage can.

"But you slept through the dog raiding the fridge," she pointed out.

"Different kind of racket. Besides, I was exhausted by then. You didn't hear him either."

She felt a shiver of pure appreciation. The light from the window, muted and watery, was falling around him. He was dressed for work in jeans faded nearly white, the fabric worn to threads just below the back pocket. He had on a navy T-shirt, much like the one she had discarded, and he had not tucked it in. Both items of clothing were old and soft, melting against the lines of his body—the jeans hugging the hard length of long legs and the steely curve of his buns, the shirt clinging to the broad sweep of his back and shoulders.

His feet were bare, and it struck her, absurdly, as being wonderfully intimate to be standing in a kitchen with him in his bare feet. Okay, it smelled like pickles, and not coffee, and he could hurt himself on a stray piece of glass, but it was still a lovely moment. She wished she had her camera.

He glanced back at her, and his eyes lingered just long enough to make her glad she had chosen the sweater. He looked swiftly back to the dustpan, set it aside and got a rag from the kitchen sink. He began to swab up the floor.

"It wasn't just you that kept me awake. The dog snores. And sighs. And growls. And whimpers. And groans. And changes position. All just a big ruse to make me think he's sleeping, so he can raid the fridge. Bad Basil."

The dog sighed heavily.

Ty tossed the rag in the sink and began spooning coffee into his coffeemaker. "You like your coffee strong?"

The morning light illuminated the line of his arm, and she noticed the unconscious ripple of the muscle in his forearm every time he moved. She decided she liked her men strong and her coffee weak.

"That will be fine the way it is," she said. Her voice sounded breathless, like an adolescent girl in the presence of her current heartthrob.

"About that kiss," he said, taking a deep breath and addressing the real reason they had both tossed and turned until three in the morning.

She glared at his broad back. "Don't mention it," she said stiffly. *Not one word, in fact.* But could the fact he was mentioning it first thing in the morning, in between dealing with a disaster and making coffee, before he even had his socks on, be in any way meaningful?

He said, "You've changed. I don't think I've ever seen one person change so much. Your hair, your glasses, even your teeth."

"Ugly duckling to swan," she said, with forced lightness, hurt that he remembered all of her deficiencies so accurately.

"Obviously, I didn't know who you were," he went on.

"Much better manners to kiss strangers than someone you know," she agreed, her voice just sweet enough to hide her annoyance.

He turned and glanced at her again, this time looking distinctly irritated. "I don't kiss my sister's friends."

"A rule that must have made perfect sense when your sister was a child," she said, then realized that could sound like an invitation. "Not that I'm suggesting in any way that I wanted that to happen. Or encouraged it. Or would ever want it to happen again."

This was the type of thing that had gotten Pinocchio in such dreadful trouble.

"Good," he said, with tight-lipped satisfaction. "I just wanted to make sure we were on the same page."

"Oh, definitely," she said, in her worldly photographer voice, "the very same page."

Secretly she felt angry. She would have liked to test his control! She had to fight the most compelling temptation to make it happen all over again, to fling herself at him, to take his bottom lip between her teeth and dissolve the firm line of it.

"It was hardly even a kiss," she said, using her most worldly tone.

"I don't do things like that." His voice was a low, embarrassed growl. "Why did you lie to me about your name? Why didn't you just tell me who you were?"

"I didn't lie to you about my name. I got married."

"You're married?" His voice sounded strangled, upset.

"Not anymore," she said.

"Oh. I'm sorry." But he didn't sound the least bit sorry. He sounded relieved.

"I had the shortest marriage in history," she blurted out, then felt ridiculous for wanting to tell him, for wanting to share it with him, as if he, of all people, would understand.

He looked at her, long and hard and steady. She could tell by the light in his eyes that he would understand. She could tell that he wanted to know.

And she could tell he was at war with himself. They stood at a turning point: move closer together or farther away. He sucked a deep breath of air in between his perfect white teeth, and she held her breath.

"Look, Harriet, I think the best thing would be if we could get this over with as quickly as possible."

For a full second she misunderstood what he had said. She thought he had chosen door number one:

Let's explore this tension between us, get it out of the way as quickly as possible so we can get to the work at hand.

Then she realized that wasn't what he meant at all. Like her, he sensed the danger in the air, the sexual tension between them. His choice was to walk away from it, focus on the work at hand. He wanted her out of his hair and his house. His hair was sleep ruffled, a little rooster tail springing up at the back. She had an urge to go smooth it into place.

"Agreed," she squeaked. "Let's get it over with."

"So, you tell me what I need to do for you to get those calendar pictures, and I'll do it. Full cooperation."

Anything to get rid of her. She was a nuisance. Annoying. Nothing at all had changed since that summer when she was first here, had first seen him, had first fallen.

Unless…there was a different light in his eyes. Was there the faintest chance she had power over him? That he found her attractive?

The temptation was to play with that power, and maybe a woman more sure of herself would have. But Harriet, confident in almost every aspect of her life, knew herself to be terrible at the man–woman thing.

She would end up being the victim of such a game, not him. She could not toy with the electricity that sizzled in the air between them without being singed by it. She could leave here this time in much worse shape than she had left here last time if she was not very, very careful.

"All right," she said, crisp and professional. "I'd like to get the Christmas shot out of the way first. I see out the window it looks like it's going to rain. Bad light, raindrops on the camera lens. If we could do interior shots today that might work best."

"I need to do chores and get the guys organized for

the day. It'll take me about an hour, and then I'm all yours.'' Apparently he realized his meaning could be mistaken, because he turned back to the coffee machine and drummed his fingers while it dripped.

"Perfect," she said, thinking of those adolescent hours she had spent looking at the photographs she had taken of him, dreaming of hearing words like *I'm all yours*. None of that girl in the voice that said, "I need an hour or so to set up the shot. And would you mind not shaving? Or combing your hair?"

She knew every woman who saw that little rooster tail would think of her fingers in the smooth, dark silk of his hair.

But Ty cast a disbelieving look at her. "Women dream about spending Christmas morning with a slob? No wonder I'm such a dead loss with the female half of the species."

"You're a dead loss with the female species?" she repeated, incredulous.

"Oh, you know. Never know what to say. Bored after ten minutes of hand holding and eye gazing. You know."

She knew *she* felt like that. But him? Looking at him, morning rumpled, with the whiskers darkening on his cheeks and his hair standing up in cute little spikes, she knew what he did not: a woman would never look at him and see a slob. He looked sexy and mysterious and vaguely dangerous. And a woman would never be bored after ten minutes of hand holding and eye gazing with him, either.

Harriet needed to capture, on film, that exact look he was giving her, a sidelong glance from under his lashes, his mouth faintly quirked. She needed to capture, on film, the sexual tension that sizzled in the room between them—without giving in to it.

"You'd be surprised what women like," Harriet said, trying to drain from her voice just how much they liked it.

"Oh, yeah. I have a feeling I'm in for a lot of surprises."

She bet he'd be surprised if she went over there, wrapped her hands in his T-shirt, pulled him to her and kissed him senseless.

She had to quit thinking thoughts like this! They were like renegades, storming the walls of a brain that had always been perfectly professional and perfectly proper.

She was on a mission, she reminded herself sternly. To capture his essence and his charm, without succumbing to either. She was here to prove to herself that Tyler Jordan was a girlhood infatuation that she had outgrown.

She made her sluggish brain form words that had nothing to do with kisses. "We'll do the Christmas shots," she said, taking charge, needing to be the boss, needing control, "and then I could do some interior shots in the barn. You brushing a horse or throwing some hay. I could pass those off as winter scenes, since we don't have snow."

"The horses don't have their winter coats," he pointed out uncooperatively.

"Believe me, most people don't know that."

"Well, I do and I'm not going to look like an idiot on thousands of calendars, thanks."

Somebody had forgotten to give him the instruction book. Being the boss meant it went your way. "Is this your idea of being cooperative?"

"You can't give people horses with spring coats, and tell them it's winter," he said stubbornly. "Doesn't the word *integrity* have any meaning in your world?"

She flinched. "And what world is that?"

"The public relations world," he said.

"Do I detect a hint of scorn?"

He shrugged. "I just don't get it. Women like you and Stacey using your energy to create a world where every kid believes he doesn't have value unless he had the right brand name on his sneakers. A world where dancing rabbits sell toilet paper. A world where talking dogs make little kids drive their moms wild for games that they'll play with once before they think the box is more fun. Is that any way to use your life?"

She had worked with men under harsh conditions for a long time. She kept a handle on her emotions. So she could not believe it when she felt as if she might cry. "My life is not about selling toilet paper," she said, softly and clearly, "it is about creating images of lasting beauty."

He looked surprised. "Oh, geez. I wasn't talking about you. I was talking about Stacey dating a hippie. She could have done anything, and instead she ends up in this world of hype and plastic where nothing is quite real."

Oh. He was talking about Stacey. Was he seeing her as the woman who had led his little sister astray? Into the big bad world of plastic and hype?

Don't let it get personal, she warned herself.

Haughtily Harriet said, "We're not rewriting the cowboy code of honor here. We're creating an illusion. It's like working on a movie set. And Stacey's boyfriend is not a hippie just because he has long hair."

"I've hurt your feelings," he said, looking at her more closely than she liked, seeing exactly what she thought she had so successfully hidden. "I told you. Terrible at the man–woman thing."

Back to that. The man–woman thing. Between them. Even if she was Stacey's friend...who had led her astray.

"Just smile for the camera," she said, "and if I do my job right nobody will ever guess that you're terrible at the man–woman thing. My specialty, as you've said—creating irresistible illusions. World's crankiest man to world's sexiest male in the click of a shutter."

"World's crankiest? Really?" He looked rather pleased.

"Try to think of the next few days like making a movie," she suggested again.

He gave her the cranky guy look, and became impatient with waiting for his coffee to finish. He took the coffeepot out from under the drip and held his coffee cup there. When it was full he deftly switched the two and headed for the door. "See you in an hour or so."

"Wait! I'll need, um, props. Do you have any Christmas decorations?"

"Under the stairs."

"And how about socks? You know, to hang on the hearth?"

He rolled his eyes. "In my dresser drawer. Help yourself."

She did not really care for the idea of rifling through his dresser drawers, but given his eagerness to get away from her, she could see he was not going to help.

"I'll grab something to eat at the bunkhouse. I'd invite you, but you don't want to see those guys in the morning. There's cereal and toast and stuff in the cupboards. Make yourself at home."

She suspected the real truth was that Ty Jordan did not want to spend any more time in her presence than he had to, though debating whether it was because she sold toilet paper for a living or whether it was because he found her unbelievably attractive was the type of question that would drive her crazy.

After making herself some toast and sampling one sip of his coffee, which was thick and dark and bitter, she turned to the living room.

She closed the drapes against the rain and looked around. It was a humbly furnished room, but the blue-checkered armchair was homey and cheerful. She shoved it over by the fireplace, a magnificent structure constructed of river rock. She placed the few lights, working with them until she got exactly the nice soft glow she was looking for.

Growing more content by the minute, she went and found the box of Christmas decorations. She hung a holly garland on the mantel. Though it was plastic, she knew with the right light, and work in the darkroom, she could make it appear real. She found some wrapping paper and bows and wrapped a box. The firewood was in a container beside the hearth, and she carefully built a fire, ready to strike a match to it when he came back.

A few socks tacked to that lovely oak mantel and the picture would be complete.

She went into his bedroom with trepidation, feeling like a Peeping Tom, feeling like that teenage girl, dying to collect little tidbits about him to store in her little memory box that she could haul out and sift through in the future.

Except it was going to be totally different this time, she reminded herself. And it might have been, if his room had been a room that showed power and assurance, that looked like the room of a man who could have any woman he wanted. It might have been easy to begin strengthening the wall around her heart and psyche if he'd had a four-poster bed and a heavy walnut bureau and if everything shone and proclaimed masculine strength and force, and if it looked like a room a thousand women had been seduced in.

But his room was nothing like that.

It underscored the truth of what he had said. He would be terrible at the man–woman thing.

Ty Jordan's bedroom was a room without romance, without one single ounce of appeal. There was a double bed, made hastily, with gray blankets and plain white sheets and pillow covers. A scarred bureau was up against the wall opposite to the bed. There was a brush on top of the bureau and a few socks drifting out the bottom drawer. And that was it for the furnishings.

There were no pictures on the walls, no matching bed-spread and pillow shams, no trinkets on the dresser, not even a rug on the hardwood floor.

To Harriet the room seemed unbearably lonely, and it did the worst possible thing to her.

It made her see Tyler, not as the man nine out of ten women could love, but as a man dying of his own lone-liness, vulnerable.

And apparently blissfully unaware of his condition, she reminded herself.

Hardening her heart, which was the mission, she marched across the room and opened the top drawer. Pe-ripherally she registered she had already seen socks in the bottom one.

The top drawer contained T-shirts, shoved in, unfolded. The middle drawer was completely empty. The third one contained underwear, boxers not jockeys, not that it was any of her business, and not that she should be blushing about it.

The socks she was looking for were in the bottom of the dresser, and she found several that were perfect: old-fashioned ugly gray wool socks with white toes and heels that would look perfect hung with care on the mantel.

After hanging the socks, she stood back and again felt

pleased. All the picture needed was a cup of hot chocolate on the corner of that coffee table. Real hot chocolate would be a disaster because it would melt the whipping cream, though chances of his having whipping cream were slim anyway.

She got a heavy masculine-looking mug from the kitchen, and after some thought filled it with shaving cream from his bathroom cabinet. The foamy white peaks looked perfectly delicious, and were guaranteed to last however long the shoot took.

As a final touch she retrieved Basil from his exile outside and brought him in. He scorned the big bowl of dog food at the back door and went right to the fridge. He would not budge from the fridge door until she produced a snack. She gave him a slice of lunch meat, and when that failed to take the mournful look off his face, she also found gave him some more of the cheese he had enjoyed earlier—this time without the plastic wrap.

Then she fashioned a huge red bow for his neck, ordered him to sit and retrieved her camera from her bedroom. When she came back, Basil had managed to get into the fridge again. He was happily lapping broken raw eggs off the floor.

"You are a bad dog," she said as she mopped up the mess.

His big red-rimmed eyes looked appropriately contrite. He licked a little eggshell off his muzzle.

"Okay," she conceded, "cute but bad. Very bad."

"Who's cute but bad?" Ty said from the mudroom.

Oh, God, don't even ask. She told herself her job necessitated her looking at him so intently.

Her job necessitated her finding what it was in him that would make nine out of ten women want to find him under their Christmas tree.

"Have you got pajamas?" she asked him. His hair was damp from being outside. The effect was even better than the rooster tails. It looked as if he had just come from the shower.

"Pajamas?" he echoed, coming up the stairs into the kitchen, and staring at her as if she had asked him to produce a thong.

"You know, flannel. Plaid." Cute but bad.

"I don't wear pajamas."

How was that for cute but bad? Harriet could feel her face burning. How was this turning so personal? Now she was wondering what he wore to bed! And she was hoping it was nothing, as if that was any of her business.

"How about a robe?" she asked, her voice firm, professional, a woman completely uninterested in what he wore to bed.

"Yeah, Stacey gave me one last year for Christmas."

Apparently not his favorite gift of all time.

"I asked for a new tire wrench," he said grumpily.

"Do you think you could put on the robe," she asked, "over a pair of shorts? No shirt."

"Are you going to check? For the shorts?"

He was being deliberately wicked.

"Remember I'm a friend of Stacey's," she reminded him sweetly, and smiled as he stomped off to his bedroom and slammed the door.

He came back in a few minutes later, in costume, still scowling.

"This is stupid," he said, sinking down in the chair by the fire.

The robe was thick white terry cloth and long. It had a hood on it. It was obvious it had never been worn before.

It made him look sinfully sexy—if she could just get the scowling discomfort off his face. She struck a match to the fire she had laid and then took up her position with the camera. She moved around him.

"Ty, if you could just look, um, joyous."

"Like this?" His lips twisted up. The furrow remained between his eyes, which were snapping with impatience.

Ty cooperating was much worse than Ty not cooperating.

"Try opening this," she said, and tossed the wrapped package at him. "Pretend it has a tire wrench in it."

She framed the shot. It was beautiful. Fire crackling in the background. Dog and hot chocolate in the foreground, the robe gaping open just a bit above the belt to reveal the hair on his naked chest. His hair fell over his brow as he leaned over the package.

But the expression on his face! It was stiff and sour.

The fire had taken hold and was roaring away. The small room was getting uncomfortably hot. No matter how she cajoled, she could not get a genuine smile from him. The hotter it got, the more his expression became set in grim lines.

"It's Christmas for God's sake," she said. "Look happy."

"Oh, sure. I've never been happier. It's one hundred and four degrees in here and getting hotter by the second. That foul dog keeps passing wind. Pickles and cheese do not agree with his digestive system. I'll make a note of that. There is no tire wrench. This robe makes me feel like an idiot. How the hell can I look happy?"

"Can't you pretend?" she wailed. But she knew he couldn't. He was, plain and simple, a man without pretense.

And the more he tried to pretend he was happy, the further she got from the picture she wanted.

"I need a break," he said after they'd been at it a full

fifteen minutes and he'd unwrapped the parcel three times. He flung off the robe.

The faintest gleam of sweat had formed on his chest and arms.

He was in a pair of plaid boxers that made him look as sexy as any man alive. She watched through the lens as he reached for the hot chocolate, the easy ripple of the muscle in his arms mesmerizing her.

"Ty, don't—"

But it was too late. He gulped back a big mouthful of the prop. The shaving cream hit his tastebuds. His eyes crossed, he looked at her accusingly, then spit out the shaving cream, and wiped a hand across his lips.

"You're trying to poison me."

He slammed down the mug. Basil, sensing the contents were up for grabs, leaped up and sucked back every last bit of the shaving cream, then licked his lips and belched happily.

Ty sat frozen for a moment, then very slowly turned and looked at her.

He had missed a spot of shaving cream above his lip that looked exactly like whipping cream. The bright Christmas wrapping paper lay at his feet. The fire blazed merrily behind him. Basil was sniffing the mug looking for more.

And then the most incredible thing happened.

Ty laughed.

Click. In that split second, she got her Christmas picture. It was a spectacular picture—fire burning, socks on the mantel, a gorgeous man laughing at the dog who had just slurped up his hot chocolate. No one but her and Ty and the dog would ever know the real story.

But the cost to her heart of experiencing that easy laughter was tremendous. She could feel it trying to tear out of her body and go to him. She could hear her mind telling her, *I knew that's who he really was.*

She wondered how she was going to survive. She looked at Basil. "Is there poison control for dogs?" she asked.

"This is what I remember about you," he said softly.

She held her breath.

"Disaster. Lady Disaster," he informed her, and then took the sting out of it completely by saying, "Harriet Pendleton, you do what no one on earth has ever made me do. You make me laugh."

Chapter Five

Now he'd gone and done it. It was almost worse than kissing her, telling her she was the only one who made him laugh.

The kiss, after all, could be put down to a function of biology.

But laughter was something quite different. Laughter was getting into that murky area of emotion. And telling her he didn't laugh much was like admitting his life lacked certain elements. She might mistakenly think he was lonely. And cranky. And vulnerable.

All of which he was, now that he thought about it. The fact that he had not thought about it *at all* before Harriet Pendleton had arrived on his doorstep caused him to feel deep resentment. What if those guarded places in himself showed up in her stupid pictures, and the whole world saw what he really was?

Pathetic.

A man whose life was about cattle and horses and whose idea of a good time was spending a night playing cards with three disgusting men and talking about football stats. Or baseball. Or hockey, depending what time of year it was.

If he wasn't careful, he was going to end up just like those men in the bunkhouse. Old. Disgusting. Alone.

Only days ago, Ty thought, resentment deepening, he had never entertained such thoughts. Ever. He had certainly not ever thought of himself as pathetic.

It was her fault, and she had to go.

Those long legs, and flashing eyes were just a little too much for a man who lived alone. The lips, full, pouty, begged to be kissed. Begged.

And she hadn't found him disgusting or pathetic last night, not from the way she'd responded. Ty was annoyed with himself for actually feeling momentary relief that he had not crossed over the line to true bachelorhood yet.

"Okay," he said getting up decisively, "next shot. The barn you said?"

"What about Basil?" she asked worriedly.

Why didn't he just tell her what he thought? He had a backhoe. If the disgusting dog bit the dust, he could dig a hole big enough to dispose of him in about thirty seconds.

See? It was already out of hand. Because he didn't want her to know what a hard-hearted barbarian he could be. What was that all about?

"I'm going to get dressed," he said. "Vet's number is by the phone."

"Put on the jeans you had on earlier," she said. "The ones, um, a few threads short in the rear end. And the white T-shirt."

"Can I comb my hair now?" he asked sarcastically.

She missed the sarcasm, narrowed her golden-brown

eyes on his hair as if he was a bug under glass, then said, "Leave it for now."

He went into this bedroom and slammed the door. He debated putting on his darkest, newest jeans, and a black T-shirt, just to show her who was boss. But if he did that she might end up being here for an extra day or two, and that was out of the question. Even an extra hour was going to be dangerous to spend with Harriet Pendleton, and not because of the disasters either.

When the hell had she become so beautiful? And how?

And what the hell did she mean about a few threads short in the rear? He picked the jeans up off his floor and inspected them. The rear was worn right through, just below the pocket, a few threads all that were between him and the world.

He actually felt a blush moving up his cheeks. A blush! Harriet Pendleton had seen his underwear—and wanted to show it to every other woman in the Western Hemisphere! Did women like guys who were poor? Who walked around with holes in embarrassing places in their clothes? What color of underwear was he supposed to put on, now that he knew it showed?

White, he decided after some debate. That would show the least.

He hated what his world was becoming.

Get rid of her, he told himself firmly. If that means putting on jeans with a hole in the ass, that's the price. He pulled on the white underwear and the jeans. What did he care if people wanted to get a glimpse of his undies? It was a weird world out there. Which was why he lived here, on a quiet piece of land, far from the mainstream. It was just a coincidence that every single thing on this property was under his control.

Still, he had enough cowboy in him that he couldn't

just completely knuckle under to her, so in an act of rebellion that struck him as piteous, he combed his hair. And not to impress her with his good grooming habits, either. Just to let her know who was in control around here. Just to let her know.

He strode back into the living room. For a guy in control, he was certainly trying to keep his backside facing the wall.

She was sitting on the floor, long legs folded under her, and she had that giant dog's head on her lap and was stroking his big forehead with gentle fingers. Basil was sighing with contentment.

Ty wondered what her fingers would feel like on his forehead, what it would feel like to come home after a hard day on the range and put his head on her lap and look up into the liquid gold of her eyes.

Get rid of her, he reminded himself sternly. Thoughts like that would melt his resolve like instant coffee hitting hot water. He was a disciplined man. His whole life had been about discipline. Keep going even when it hurts. In fact, the harder life hurt, the faster you had to go, to outrun all that pain.

Looking at her, it was easy to imagine stopping, laying his head down, letting some hard-held control go. A woman who could give a dog that kind of sympathy could probably be trusted with a man's hurts.

Ha! Not in his lifetime.

"Is it too much to hope the dog isn't going to survive?" he asked.

It had the exact effect he wanted. She cradled the dog's head protectively and sent him a dirty look.

"I'm not sentimental about animals," he said, nailing the lid on his coffin with satisfaction. Now this was control! Look at the fighting-mad light in her eyes. "Did

Stacey tell you I hunt? The deer compete with the cattle for grub. Bambi's on my hit list.''

She gave him a look that let him know Bambi killers were safe from her affection and said haughtily, ''The vet said Basil should be fine, but that we should keep an eye on him. We might have to induce vomiting.''

''We? I don't think so, lady.''

''I'll do it if I have to.''

He didn't like it that she was genuinely worried about that unpleasant beast. He didn't like what worry did to her face, softening all the lines of it, making her look exactly how she'd looked when she was here last—all anxious and worried, as if she was constantly bracing for an earthquake or some other major catastrophe.

She was so wrapped up in the dog that she didn't appear to notice he had defied her by combing his hair.

''That dog could eat the tires off the tractor and not die from it,'' he said, giving just a little, not wanting her to like it here, but not wanting *that* look to stay on her face, either.

She failed to look reassured, and the dog was taking big gulps of air and swallowing, looking very much as if he was going to induce his own vomiting at any moment.

He had the uncharitable thought that being covered in the recycled contents of the dog's stomach might dampen her sympathy somewhat, but he didn't want to test the theory on his living room floor.

He went and wrestled the dog out of her grasp, hefted him in his arms and bolted for the door. Too late he remembered he didn't want her looking at his vulnerable backside. He glanced back and scowled at her for looking.

She actually blushed!

The heat in this house was unbearable, and it no longer had a thing to do with the fireplace!

He set the dog down, and they both stood outside the back door taking great and steadying breaths of the pure, damp air.

"She has the same effect on me, buddy," he told the dog. "Not that I want you getting any ideas about being my buddy. In fact, you can spend the day right here, tied to this—"

"Oh, you're not going to tie him up are you?"

Ty looked at the chain in his hand, resisted the impulse to put it behind his back. He reminded himself he *wanted* her to think he was a coldhearted, ruthless, dog-hating, Bambi-killing man. "Yeah, I'm tying him up."

"Oh, you shouldn't."

He straightened and looked at her. Her arms were loaded down with *his* stuff. All his winter clothes had been removed from the pegs behind the back door and were now in her arms. She also had his good black cowboy hat.

"That's not a barn hat," he said, dragging the dog over and snagging it from her. He brushed it carefully.

"What kind of hat is it?" she asked, as if she found it amusing that cowboy hats had distinctive and different functions.

"It's a special occasion hat," he said, feeling stubborn.

"Special occasion? Like a barn dance or something?"

Where had she learned about ranch life? From Walt Disney?

"Yeah, something like that," he said. She didn't need to know the truth at all. He didn't need her wondering what it said about his world that the last special occasion he had been to had been the funeral of an eighty-six-year-old neighbor.

"Could we use it for the pictures? Since you combed your hair?"

He should have known there would be a price for that small victory.

"We'll be careful. If we damage your hat, we can buy you a new one out of the calendar budget."

Was she mocking him? Did she think he was a hick because he had a special hat for special occasions? What the hell did he care what she thought? He shoved the hat on his head, pulled the brim down over his eyes just in case she was trying to guess if he cared what she thought.

"It would be better if Basil came with us. So we could keep an eye on him."

Ty really didn't think it was going to be that much fun to watch Basil unload the contents of his stomach, but one thing he had learned from Stacey, don't argue with a woman when she had that soft, mushy look on her face.

He shoved the hat on his head, remembered his rear end, and beckoned her to go down the path ahead of him.

"Hayloft," she said when they got to the barn. Once again he tried to get rid of the dog. The corner post on the paddock fence beside the barn looked as if it would hold even Basil.

"Oh, don't you think we should bring him with us? In case he gets sick?"

"Frankly, if he gets sick I want to be in the next county."

"You might have to give him mouth-to-mouth," she said.

He looked at her sharply to see if she was kidding. She wasn't, as far as he could tell. "If you think, for one second, I'd put my mouth on those big, fat slobbery lips—"

She was smiling now, and he knew she had baited him. He didn't like it when she smiled. Not one little bit. She had little white teeth, like shiny Chiclets, and a pink tongue that she had caught between them.

He led the way, hustled Basil up the steps to the loft, remembering at the last minute to drop a casual hand over the hole in his pants. Was that a little snicker from behind him? But when he turned and looked at her, she was carefully navigating the steep steps.

Dim light filtered through the loft. There was a strong support beam in the center of it, and he tied Basil to it.

"He'll probably pull the barn down on top of us," Ty predicted sourly. Come to think of it the barn coming down sounded preferable to an afternoon spent smiling and trying to keep his rear end from gaining public notoriety. Of course, now that Ty actually wanted the barn pulled down, the dog flopped down without protest, put his enormous head on his huge paws and sighed.

Unfortunately, it looked like he was going to live.

Ty folded his arms over his chest, looked back at her. She had set down her pile of clothes and was studying the loft. She took out her light meter, squinted, did readings. Finally, she turned to him. She was wearing tight jeans and a green sweater that was going to be hell to get hay out of.

Not that she was planning on rolling around in the hay. Not that he was planning on rolling her around in the hay, either!

"Could you quit scowling and put on the plaid mackinaw?"

"I'm not scowling," he muttered. The coat in question was pure wool, and he only wore it on the coldest days of the year, when the thermometer plunged to twenty or thirty below zero and the wind was howling in from the north. As soon as he put it on, he could feel the heat. *Now* he was scowling.

He reminded himself that this was part of getting her on her way down the road that led off the Bar ZZ. He smiled.

"Oh, this is perfect," she said. She'd found a hay fork. He couldn't help but think that was a lot of enthusiasm for a hay fork. "Can you pitch some hay? I know! Why don't we open the loft door, and make it look like you're pitching hay down there?"

At least having the loft door open provided the smallest of breezes. Feeling like an absolute fool, he forked some hay and posed in the loft door.

"Ty, don't look so stiff. Relax. Can you actually toss it down there?"

He glared at her. "Oh, sure," he said. Of course, everything that went down had to come back up, but what did that matter if it moved him a few seconds forward in his mission to rid his ranch of one red-headed witch?

Enchantress, a treacherous voice in his head reminded him.

Making him feel things he didn't want to feel at all. All hot and bothered, and self-conscious as a grade-seven boy at his first junior high school dance.

The hay suddenly seemed very appealing. He forked it out the door with a vengeance, after a while even managing to forget the constant whir of her camera and protecting his back end from unwanted public exposure.

After a few minutes of moving hay for her, he started to debate just jumping out the loft door. There was enough hay out there that he'd probably just break a leg. That should be the end of his modeling career.

Not to mention running his ranch for the next few months.

"Can you smile?" she pleaded.

He stopped and stared at her. He was thinking of breaking his own leg to get away from her, and she wanted him to smile?

"Smile?" he repeated, with all the tight control he could manage. "Smile? I feel like I'm in a sauna and somebody just threw another dipperful of water on the rocks. I'm throwing perfectly good hay on the ground, and I'm going to have to go down there and get it after. No man in his right mind would be smiling right now. Take the damn picture."

"Can't you think of something that would make you happy?"

"That would be strangling you."

"Uh, maybe we should move on to something else."

"Such as?" Kissing her again might make him happy. And then again, it might not. It hadn't last time. Short-term pleasure. Long-term mental chaos.

"How about these bales over here? Can you lift them? We'll trade jackets."

She handed him his fleece-lined jean jacket, and he tossed his other one off and shrugged into the new one. While she changed films, he took off his hat and regarded it sorrowfully. It had never seen hay or dust before and now it was covered with both.

He slid her a glance. He was satisfied to see the green sweater wasn't faring that well, either.

"Okay," she said, aiming the camera at him. "If they're not too heavy, lift one and walk toward me."

He snorted, lifted one bale up in each hand, and came toward her.

"If you can't look happy," she said, backing away, "could you at least look less menacing?"

"I wasn't aware I looked menacing," he said, and ex-perienced a deepening of the sensation of being self-conscious. He hated it. He could feel the menacing expression deepen.

She sighed, and let the camera slide down on her neck. "Let's try this." She came over and reached up, tugged the cowboy hat down ridiculously low over his brow. "Okay, walk toward me again, only look down at the floor. Think about something pleasant."

"Like this being over?"

"Or a big juicy steak with fries on the side. And a chocolate sundae."

Or her lips under his, soft and full of surrender.

"Oh, that's it," she breathed, and the camera shutter clicked and spoiled the mood entirely.

"Look at that goofy dog," he said, so that she would quit looking at him just for a minute, so that he could make all his thoughts private again.

She glanced over at Basil and then smiled, and then laughed out loud. A group of barn kittens had found him, and were now crawling all over him. He looked content and unperturbed. He had one between huge paws and he was giving it a thorough licking.

The camera turned away from him just like that and onto Basil. She moved around the dog quietly and clicked away.

It was insulting, really, that the dog was so much more comfortable with the camera than he was. But the truth was, Ty liked watching her work, her movements so fluid, her concentration so focused.

After a while she put down the camera and went and flung herself down in the hay with the kittens and Basil. City girl. She had no idea what it was going to take to get the hay out of that sweater.

Ty hesitated and then went and picked the camera up.

He looked at it carefully, figured it wasn't that different from his 35 mm and then took a few pictures of her.

She looked gorgeous. Hay tangled in her hair, kitten on her breast, that big dog looking at her with naked adoration.

"Come see this one, Ty." She was holding up a kitten, her eyes shining, her voice breathless with laughter.

"Nah."

"Come on. He's crabby, just like you. Look at him scowling!"

He inched over.

"Oh, they're so cute. Don't you think they're adorable?"

"I think they'll grow up and kill mice," he said flatly.

Without warning she leaped up beside him, laughingly thrust the kitten at him and grabbed her camera.

He held the kitten at arm's length and looked at it. The silly thing did have a ferocious look on its face. It batted at him with a small paw.

"Tough guy, eh?" he said. The kitten felt warm, his black fur silky. Ty, though he really knew better, tucked it into his chest and stroked the furrow between its scowling brow with his thumb.

The kitten seemed to mull this over, then relaxed against him and began to purr and butt at his chest with its damp nose. It grabbed a piece of jacket and began to suck vigorously.

"He's looking for his mama," he said, and smiled.

Click.

"I think we've got one," she said. "January or November."

Great. The whole world was going to see him cavorting in the hay with kittens as though he had nothing better to do with his life.

But at the moment he felt strangely relaxed, as if he really didn't have anything better to do with his life. He sat down in the hay and then lay back, let the kittens roam over him.

"Put down that confounded camera for a few minutes," he said. "Your model needs a break. Who would've ever guessed a man could break a sweat doing something so dumb as having his picture taken?"

One of the kittens moved confidently up his chest, placed its paws on his neck and licked his chin.

He laughed out loud, and then his eyes met hers, and he found himself patting the hay beside him. Speaking of dumb.

"Take a break, Harriet."

She hesitated, then put down the camera and came over and sank down in the hay beside him. Way too close.

He could smell the scent of her, feel the heat of her leg where it was nearly touching his. He handed her a kitten and felt a deep ache.

For all things feminine. For a woman who talked baby talk to a new kitten and held it unselfconsciously at her breast, who cooed and let it suck on her fingers.

His life had become about things hard. Hard men. Hard work. Hard hours. Hard conditions.

Having all this softness right there beside him made him feel weak with wanting something else for himself.

Don't ask her anything personal, he ordered himself sternly. But looking at her like that, her face alight, her eyes soft and dreamy, he couldn't believe there was a man out there who had ever had her and then let her go.

"So the marriage thing didn't work out, huh?"

She ducked her head and buried her cheek against the white fur of a kitten. "No," she said, her voice smooth and uncaring and not matching her body language at all. "It didn't work out."

None of his business, he told himself firmly. She obviously didn't want to talk about it. He didn't want to know.

"Why not?" Yup, that would be his voice, all right.

"Oh," she said, "it's a long story and a boring one."

"You can't take any more pictures until I stop sweating, anyway. My nose will be all shiny."

She laughed a little uncertainly. "It's a common enough story. I was terrible at being married."

"What? You were married all by yourself? You were terrible at it, but he was wonderful at it?"

He hated how he felt right now. That she had belonged to someone else. He was, in some way that he could not explain and was not proud of, glad it had not worked out.

"It didn't last very long," she said. "A couple of months. He was an actor. Zorro Snow. Have you heard of him?"

"Nah. I don't go to movies."

"He never made movies. He acted on a soap opera."

"Well, I never saw one of those, either."

"It's refreshing to meet someone who's never heard of him."

"What would make you marry an actor?" he asked. He wasn't quite sure, but it seemed to him Harriet would need a real man. What was real about a man who pretended to be somebody else for a living?

On the other hand, she specialized in make-believe, too. That should have made them suited for each other, not that he was any kind of expert on that kind of stuff. There was some other reason it hadn't worked out.

He could see in her face that she carried the weight of

it, that somehow she had allowed herself to be lessened by the failure of her marriage.

"I was young and foolish," she said, but he did not believe the lightness in her tone. "He was good looking and he made a fuss over me, and it just sort of bowled me over."

"You couldn't believe a man would make a fuss over you?" he asked. "Why?"

"Oh, Ty. That buck-toothed, freckled girl with the glasses that you met all those years ago is right inside of me telling me I'm too tall and too skinny and ugly and no one will ever love me."

She blushed wildly and stood up so fast a kitten dropped off her, mewling its indignation.

"Now why did I say that?" she said. "I hate being around you."

"You do?" He stood up, too, putting down his kitten more gently. "Why? Am I that difficult?"

"It's not because of that. It's because you make me feel like that girl all over again. I blurt out the most stupid things around you. 'No one will ever love me.' How pathetic. I didn't mean it."

"He should have loved you, Harriet. He didn't know what he had."

"What he had was an ice maiden. It wasn't his fault."

"You? An ice maiden?"

She nodded, stiff and proud. "That's right. There. Now you have the truth about why my marriage failed. Are you happy? I'm frigid. A complete failure in that department. Let's get back to work, shall we? Before I blurt out my every life secret."

He felt this slow, burning anger start in him. He looked at her copper hair and her flashing eyes and remembered the soft willingness of her lips on his last night.

Frigid?

If Zorro Snow was in the hayloft right now, he felt he could kill him with his bare hands. An actor—who had somehow made her believe she was responsible for his inadequacies.

"You're not frigid," he said.

"Thanks," she said, her voice too bright, too brittle. "I'm sure you're an expert. Let's try that scarf with the jean jacket. That should look—"

"Harriet," he said, taking her shoulders between his hands, making her look at him. "You are not frigid. You hear?"

Her eyes went very wide. She licked her lips nervously. And yet she was looking at him desperately, as if he could throw her a lifeline.

There were times when a man had to put his own instinct for self-preservation on hold. There were times when he had to do what was right, even if it was at great personal cost to himself.

And what was right in this instant, they both knew.

He leaned toward her, and she leaned toward him. He took the fullness of her bottom lip between his teeth and gnawed it gently.

She melted. Not ice at all, just as he had known, but fire.

She melted against him, the soft curves of her breasts becoming one with the hard line of his chest. Even through the thickness of the jacket, he could feel her nipples tighten, sense her breath coming harder.

He parted her lips with his tongue, moved inside, felt her fire.

She wrapped her arms around his neck, pulled him hard to her.

It occurred to him, woozily, he had not thought this

Play the
LUCKY
Carnival Wheel
Game....
GET YOUR
3 GIFTS
FREE !
PLAY FOR
FREE !
NO PURCHASE
NECESSARY !

How To Play:

1. With a coin, carefully scratch off the 3 gold areas on your Lucky Carnival Wheel. By doing so you have qualified to receive everything revealed—2 FREE books and a surprise gift—ABSOLUTELY FREE!

2. Send back this card and you'll receive 2 brand-new Silhouette Romance® novels. These books have a cover price of $3.99 each in the U.S. and $4.50 each in Canada, but they are yours ABSOLUTELY FREE.

3. There's no catch! You're under no obligation to buy anything. We charge nothing—ZERO—for your first shipment. And you don't have to make any minimum number of purchases— not even one!

4. The fact is thousands of readers enjoy receiving books by mail from the Silhouette Reader Service™. They enjoy the convenience of home delivery…they like getting the best new novels at discount prices, BEFORE they're available in stores… and they love their *Heart to Heart* subscriber newsletter featuring author news, horoscopes, recipes, book reviews and much more!

5. We hope that after receiving your free books you'll want to remain a subscriber. But the choice is yours—to continue or cancel, any time at all! So why not take us up on our invitation, with no risk of any kind. You'll be glad you did!

A surprise gift

FREE

We can't tell you what it is…but we're sure you'll like it! A

FREE GIFT!

just for playing LUCKY CARNIVAL WHEEL!

Visit us online at
www.eHarlequin.com

LUCKY Carnival Wheel

Find Out Instantly The Gifts You Get Absolutely FREE!

Scratch-off Game

Scratch off ALL 3 Gold areas

YES!

I have scratched off the 3 Gold Areas above. Please send me the 2 FREE books and gift for which I qualify! I understand I am under no obligation to purchase any books, as explained on the back and on the opposite page.

315 SDL DNW9   215 SDL DNW3

FIRST NAME

LAST NAME

ADDRESS

APT.#

CITY

STATE/PROV.

ZIP/POSTAL CODE

The Silhouette Reader Service™—Here's how it works:

Accepting your 2 free books and gift places you under no obligation to buy anything. You may keep the books and gift and return the shipping statement marked "cancel." If you do not cancel, about a month later we'll send you 6 additional novels and bill you just $3.34 each in the U.S., or $3.80 each in Canada, plus 25¢ shipping & handling per book and applicable taxes if any.* That's the complete price and — compared to cover prices of $3.99 each in the U.S. and $4.50 each in Canada—it's quite a bargain! You may cancel at any time, but if you choose to continue, every month we'll send you 6 more books, which you may either purchase at the discount price or return to us and cancel your subscription.

*Terms and prices subject to change without notice. Sales tax applicable in N.Y. Canadian residents will be charged applicable provincial taxes and GST.

If offer card is missing write to: Silhouette Reader Service, 3010 Walden Ave., P.O. Box 1867, Buffalo, NY 14240-1867

BUSINESS REPLY MAIL
FIRST-CLASS MAIL   PERMIT NO. 717-003   BUFFALO, NY

POSTAGE WILL BE PAID BY ADDRESSEE

SILHOUETTE READER SERVICE
3010 WALDEN AVE
PO BOX 1867
BUFFALO NY 14240-9952

NO POSTAGE
NECESSARY
IF MAILED
IN THE
UNITED STATES

experiment through to the end. This was Harriet, his little sister's best friend. What on earth was he going to do? Lay her down in the hay and take her to the place they were both desperate to go?

No.

Not Harriet. She might say that was what she wanted, she might convince herself that was what she wanted, she might even believe it.

But he knew something about her that she did not. Just as she was not frigid, neither could she withstand the storm-tossed waters of an affair.

Oh, she thought she was worldly and sophisticated.

But her lips told him something else. She was not in the least frigid, but she was an old-fashioned girl under all that new-fangled armor.

She deserved a forever kind of man.

He had lost his faith in forever a long, long time ago. As he'd stood at the graveside of his mother, that faith had cracked, and when he had buried his father it had shattered.

Raising Stacey, after the death of his parents, had made him so aware of the pain and fear that were involved in loving—a man's total lack of control over the things he wanted to control most.

It was no mistake that he was alone on this ranch.

Ty Jordan had decided a long, long time ago he was not going to love again. Physical strength he had in abundance. Mental strength he had by the bushel.

But the kind of faith it took to lay yourself at the feet of fate and plead for mercy he did not have.

He would never have it.

He released her from his arms, and despite the heat inside that jacket, he felt ice cold, as if he was letting go of the source of all warmth when he was in the middle of an ice storm.

"Sorry," he said.

"Sorry?" she repeated.

He touched her cheek, let his hand linger for a moment, savored the downy softness of her skin, before he pulled away.

"You are fire," he told her, with quiet fierceness, "not ice." And then he turned quickly on his heel and walked away, before the heat of her beckoned for him to come in out of the cold he had walked in for so many years.

Before he surrendered.

"Which picture next?" he asked gruffly, not daring to look at her, knowing he would see tears like diamonds sparkling in her eyes.

What a fool he had been to think he was the kind of man who could fix something so delicate and complicated as a woman's heart.

Chapter Six

"No!"

Harriet was furious at this turn of events. *Which picture next?* he asked. As if he was going to kiss her like that and then just walk away? It was just too much like last time and too much like every time.

"No?" he said, and turned and regarded her with surprise, as if he expected her to be holding back tears.

How did men always end up with all the power? It came to her—a sudden illumination—that she might have a basic problem with her thought processes when it came to her approach to Ty Jordan.

She had come here to retrieve power given away. Did she think Ty was in charge of that power? Did she think he was going to offer it to her?

She had to take it. And suddenly she knew exactly how to do that.

She stalked across the hayloft after him. His eyes widened as he saw her coming. He planted himself, legs apart, arms across his chest, brows knifing downward. He looked as big as a mountain and twice as intimidating.

"Don't," he warned her.

But she was done being warned, bossed around. Tired of being told, *You're frigid* from Zorro, or *You're fire* from Ty. They were just flip sides of the same coin. Who were they to decide what *she* was? How dare they presume to do so! Harriet knew, suddenly and with certainty, she had to find out for herself who she was, know for herself what she was.

Taking a deep breath, summoning all her courage, she covered the distance between them. When she stood in the shadow of his broad shoulders, the realization crossed his features that he knew she wasn't just going to obey him.

"I'm not a puppy," she told him. "Don't you dare say 'don't' to me."

He held her gaze, then looked away to Basil. "I'm not having much luck with him, either. Not that I'm insinuating you're in the same category. At all."

It pleased her that his gargantuan confidence seemed to be failing. In fact, he unfolded his arms. He backed up a step. He looked as if he was going to turn and run. She launched herself at him, intending to wrap her arms around his midsection, pull him to her, make him surrender to the attraction between them.

But she misjudged the distance, and hit him harder than she had expected. He was already partly turned, and the force took him off guard. His knee folded under him, and he began to topple, and her momentum carried her down with him.

He wrapped his arms around her, protecting her from the fall, even though she was aware she really didn't deserve his protection. The hay cushioned them, but bits of grass and dust exploded around them as they fell into it.

She sneezed hard, three times in a row, then buried herself against his chest, utterly humiliated.

"This could only happen to me," she said. "Only I could decide to kiss a man and end up bowling him over, literally. And sneezing all over him."

It pierced her embarrassment, that it felt amazingly right to be this close to him. His body was lean underneath hers, solid as a rock. She could feel the steady deepness of his breath, the heat of him pooling deliciously where they touched. Finally, when he made no move to get out from under her, she hazarded a look up at him.

He had the look of a man shell-shocked, not exactly what the romantic in her might have been hoping for.

"Ty," she said, not knowing why, just needing to roll his name over her tongue and off her lips, needing to say it in this new way: soft, husky, full of invitation.

His hat had toppled off when she had hit him, and she took a deep breath, for courage, and then ran her fingers through his hair.

He caught her wrist. "Don't," he warned again, but there was a funny little rasp in his voice. And then he said softly, "Harriet."

She took his lips with hers. His hands came to her shoulders, hard, and she thought he was going to shove her aside.

"I've unleashed a monster," he said softly, his lips only a breath away from hers. "I think I liked it better when you thought you were frigid."

The old Harriet would have been devastated. She would have leaped to her feet and brushed off her clothes and run for the barn door. But there was a new Harriet shaking herself awake inside of her. And the new Harriet could feel the wild beat of his heart, the new Harriet could smell something wild and masculine in the air, the new Harriet could hear the desperation right behind the even tones of his voice.

The new Harriet saw right through the words, especially when she looked into his eyes. The calm was gone from them, and a storm, passionate and untamable, brewed very close to the still surface.

"You didn't like me better when I was frigid," she said, "and I can prove it."

The hands tightened on her shoulders, bit into them, and she felt the raw strength of him, knew he could dispose of her in a second. But she also felt the hesitation, and pressed it by taking his lips again, touching ever so lightly, tasting ever so gently.

His lips looked hard but they were soft. They tasted sweet and wild, and when they parted under hers, she knew the fight was over.

He groaned, and his arms slid off her shoulders, wrapped around her midriff, and he pulled her tighter into him, their bodies fused. His tongue, sensual, hot, slipped into her mouth, and she shivered as he ran the tip of it over the edge of her front teeth.

Harriet had sought power, but she had sought it naively, expecting the kind of electricity one uses to plug in their toaster, and finding instead a power beyond measure, beyond imagining.

She had discovered the power that had survived all other powers, surpassed it, that had been there at the beginning of the earth and would be there at the end.

She had inadvertently stumbled into the power of life itself: the force between a man and a woman that the very survival of the earth relied upon.

His mouth on hers showed her power that was not just

hers and not just his but something bigger than both of them, magnificent beyond comprehension, wild beyond taming, a force not to be harnessed.

She did not command this power. It commanded her. It awoke in her a hunger to know Ty that obliterated all reason. All sense, every modesty and every inhibition she had ever known was stripped from her instantly by this force she had unleashed.

The question of whether she was frigid melted in the inferno.

Her hands found their way inside his jacket, and she flattened her palms over the muscular ripples of his taut belly, let them slide slowly upward to the hard mounds of pectoral muscles. Caught in the spell of pure sensuality, she grew bolder. She slipped her fingers inside his shirt, needing to feel, to know, to discover, to explore. His skin felt like the most wondrous of miracles. It was unblemished silk, warm and resilient under her pulsating fingertips. Her breathing quickened, and so did his.

He made an effort at control, but was frozen momentarily by this new boldness. She felt his muscles tighten, sensed he wanted to pull away, to regain the lost ground of his power. She moved her hands over his breast, touched the nub of his nipple, brushed ever so lightly and felt a different kind of tension sing along his taut muscles.

Hesitation, and then his thumb, light, gentle, brushed across her breast.

She had not thought the experience could intensify, but when he touched her so intimately she had to redefine everything she had thought was true up until that moment. What she had thought was hot seemed suddenly cool, as this new level of heat unfolded within her, ran like liquid flame through her veins, sizzled along sensitive nerve endings, tingled somewhere between pleasure and pain on the surface of her skin.

His mouth caught hers again. Whatever innocence had been in that first meeting of lips was now banished. His mouth covered hers with a new force. Not brutal, but certainly not tender, either. Passion, that magnificent fury, was unleashed.

And her passion matched his, shocking in its terrible and beautiful intensity. When his lips demanded, hers answered, when his commanded, hers obeyed.

He wrapped his legs around her legs, his hands caught tight to her shoulders, and without ever lifting his lips from hers, he rolled them over. Suddenly he was on the top, his weight sweetly crushing. The hard, hot line of his thigh inserted itself between her legs, and something primal within her rose toward this unmistakable invitation.

"Boss. You in here?"

They both froze. Ty lifted himself off her, listened. She could see his heart beating, rapid and strong, through his shirt. His arms trembled slightly from holding his weight up from her.

"Boss?"

He said a word under his breath that she had heard men use many times before when they were under extreme duress. She reached up, wanting to touch the place where his heart beat, wanting to stop time, wanting him to ignore the call. He glanced at her, then pantherlike he rolled off her, landed on his feet, straightened. His chest heaving, he ran a hand through his hair, brushed at some of the hay that clung to him.

The footsteps coming up the loft stairs sounded like those of the giant in "Jack and the Beanstalk."

Harriet was having more trouble getting back to the real world than he was. She wanted to stretch out in the hay, nurse this incredible feeling inside her of the world being made up of just the two of them.

Ty reached down, and none-too-gently yanked her to her feet. His hands swift, harsh with urgency, he brushed the hay from her.

"I knew that sweater was a dumb thing to wear in a hayloft," he said.

"I'll remember that for next time." Even in her daze she noticed there was something protective about the way he ran a hand through her hair, adjusted the neckline of her sweater.

"There isn't going to be a next time," he growled.

Even so, when Slim appeared in the doorway, he shoved her behind him, as if her modesty was in need of protecting, as if she was naked, instead of just flushed and covered in hay from her hair to her toes.

"What?" Ty snapped.

Slim squinted at him, and slow comprehension spread up his face, from wrinkle to wrinkle, until it lit his eyes with a wicked light.

"It's not what you think," Ty said fiercely. "Harriet's taking pictures."

"How do you know what I think?" the man asked, amused.

Ty glared at him. "Believe me, I know how you think."

"Well, okay. Here you are, with a pretty girl in the hayloft, both of you covered in hay, cheeks flushed about the color of—"

Ty took a step forward, and Harriet noticed his fist clenched at his side.

Slim's weathered face registered surprise, and then he said, "Far as I can tell, you're both grown-ups. Ain't none of my business."

"Exactly," Ty said, tersely. "Just tell me what you want."

"Uh, we got a calving problem down in that southwest quarter. I done tried to turn the little beggar, but I ain't got the strength no more. I thought I'd better come find you."

Harriet peeked out from behind Ty and tried to read his face. It was closed and grim. Was he relieved by the rescue or regretful, or a little bit of both, just as she was?

Ty bent and retrieved his hat from the hay, slapped it against his leg and regarded the brim with an expression of woe that made Harriet want to laugh. Or maybe that desire to laugh was to break the tension that was now way too thick up here in this loft.

Even Basil seemed to feel it. He looked anxiously from one face to the other.

Slim decided, wisely, to focus on the hat. "Now, that's a shame," he said. "That's your good hat, ain't it boss?"

Ty glared at him.

"Okay, so the hat's off-limits, too," he grumbled. "I can look after the cow myself, I suppose. I just need to find the pulling chains. I think they're in the other truck, and Pete's got it and I didn't think I had time, but—"

"Never mind," Ty said, and shot her a look, "I'm coming."

"Me, too," she said, grabbing her camera. Slim turned and retreated with great haste down the stairs.

"It's good he came along when he did," Ty said gruffly.

She slung her camera around her neck and eyed Ty. "Don't think this is over," she warned him pleasantly, "because it isn't."

"Yes, it is," he said, all steely resolve.

"Says who?" she said, folding her arms over her chest.

"Says me," he said, folding his arms over his chest.

"Who put you in charge of the whole world?"

"I'm trying to be sane," he said. "And reasonable."

"You know what? I've been sane and reasonable my whole life. And I've decided not to be anymore."

"And you had to wait until you got here to make that decision?" he asked, obviously torn between irritation and amusement.

"I guess I did," she said without apology. She plucked some hay from her sweater. His eyes, hot, followed her hand.

"Why do I have all the luck?"

"Oh, in the luck department you haven't seen anything yet," she told him, delighting in this new bold self.

He didn't look nearly so pleased with the new bold self as she was. He thumped his hat down on his head hard and went down the steps two at a time in front of her.

She noticed, now that he had bigger things to worry about, that he'd forgotten all about the hole in the seat of his pants. She retrieved the dog and followed Ty out of the loft.

An old pickup truck was running outside the barn door, and Slim was already in the driver's seat. Ty looked as if he was going to say something about that, since he evidently thought his world would be safer if Slim was in the middle seat. But in the end, he just watched as she helped Basil into the back of the truck and then he held open the door for her as she slid into the middle.

"So, what's the problem?" he asked Slim, sliding in cautiously beside her. The two men were big and the cab was small, so the fact that he was not making contact with any part of her body seemed like somewhat of an engineering miracle.

She moved just slightly. Her shoulder touched his arm,

her knee brushed his thigh. He couldn't move any farther away without going out the door.

The conversation that followed was one that both men seemed totally comfortable with, while she only understood about every second word they said.

"What's a breach?" she finally interrupted. "And a heifer?"

Ty had apparently been doing his best to forget she was here, despite the pressure of her knee on his thigh. He looked out the window while Slim filled her in on calves coming out the wrong way, and first-time mama cows.

"That bull we put on her was a big boy," Slim said matter-of-factly. "The calf is probably too big for her. Gonna rip her—"

"Slim, shut up." Ty said this quietly, without looking away from the window.

"Huh?"

"He wants you to watch out for my delicate female sensibilities," Harriet whispered to Slim.

"Oh, right. Got ya, boss." He looked for a change of subject. "I threw a coil of rope in the back, just in case we have to pull that calf out of there."

"Pull him out of there? What does that mean?" she asked weakly. She was not so sure she should have been so forceful about her right to be included in this expedition. She had seen many things in her career as a photographer, and not all of them pretty. But blood and guts did her in.

"It just means we might have to help the little guy into the world," Ty said quickly, before Slim got a chance to get in a more colorful explanation.

The truck slowed down for a gate, Ty hopped out and opened it. It was the same kind of gate as before, one that required quite a bit of muscle to open. She felt herself melting inside as she watched the powerful play of his arm muscles as he wrestled the gate open, then closed it. She glanced out the window as he came back to the truck, watching the long, looseness of his stride with new eyes, with a certain possessiveness that made her tingle down to the bottom of her toes.

"Thar she is," Slim said moments later. He slammed on the brakes and cut the engine.

The two men piled out of the truck fast. Harriet followed, adjusting her camera. The cow did not look small to her.

She looked enormous, standing, her back rounded up, her bellows filling the air, her eyes wild and helpless and pain-filled.

Despite the damp in the air, Ty had his shirt off in a second. "I see hooves," he said, and then said three words in a row that would have made a sailor blush.

"What's wrong?" she said, coming as close as she dared.

"See those little black shiny things? That's his hooves. The bottom of the hoof should be pointing up toward the sky. They ain't." It was Slim who was narrating.

Without the slightest hesitation, Ty was on the ground. He inserted his arm in the cow nearly up to his shoulder. "I can feel his tail, dammit."

Slim sighed. "Upside down and backward."

"What's that mean?"

"That we're in for a rough couple of hours. Calf will probably be dead when we're through. It takes too long."

She gasped.

Ty gave Slim a dirty look. "Get her out of here. She doesn't need to see this."

"You want to go?" Slim asked, apparently a little more well versed in feminism than his boss.

She shook her head.

"The lady doesn't want to go," Slim said stubbornly. "Besides, you'll need me."

Ty glared at both of them, then turned his attention to the matter at hand. She stared at Ty, mesmerized. He had the little black hooves in his hands, and was pushing against them. She had never seen a man apply such brute strength. The muscles in his back were coiled, the cords in his neck were standing out.

"What's he doing?" she whispered.

"He's trying to push the calf back in so he can turn him around. It ain't easy—like trying to stop a river. She's pushing with everything she's got, and that's quite a bit more than what Ty's got. It can go on for a couple of hours. Calf usually dies. Can't handle the stress for that long."

She watched as Ty changed his grip, reached in, applied all his strength to the problem at hand. He was Samson—his every nerve and fibre and muscle straining against a force that was so much greater than him. There was a look on his face that said he would die before he quit, a steely resolve that made her feel weak inside.

Harriet felt a kinship with women, past and present, who had watched their men ply their great physical strength against the challenges of a world that could be cruel. She was swept with awe as she watched Ty's determination and masculine power join to create an implacable force.

The battle raged. It was a struggle like she had never seen before. After a while, she picked up her camera and began to take pictures. Ty didn't notice her, he was so intensely focused on the life-and-death drama unfolding.

The men spoke rarely, and when they did it was in a terse code.

Five minutes drifted into twenty and then an hour. She did not know how long Ty's stamina could hold. How long could a man give one hundred percent before he gave in, before he collapsed?

"Is he going to have to give up?" she asked Slim.

"Ain't in his makeup," Slim said. "'Sides, if he gave up, he'd lose both of them. We lose a calf sometimes this way, but not a cow."

"Hey, I think I might have it."

But there had been these false alarms several times already. And then the cow would push those two little feet right back out, causing Ty to wince with pain as she contracted around his arm.

"I got him," Ty said suddenly, brief jubilation lighting his features. "He's turned."

Slim brought Ty a rope. Quickly, expertly, like a man who'd done this task a thousand times before, he tied the rope around the calf's slightly protruding feet. Then he tied a loop around his own waist. He took a deep breath, marshaled his strength.

"Ty, pull," Slim shouted.

Every time the cow contracted, he leaned back hard against that rope.

The sweat was running off him in rivulets, mixed with blood and slime and mud. Harriet was not sure she had ever seen a man more beautiful, more in his element, more masculine.

"Any minute now," Slim said. "But don't get your hopes up, missy. Chances are the calf's too weak now to make it."

Five minutes. Ten. Ty's naked chest was gleaming and heaving. His hair was plastered to his forehead. The sweat flew off him and ran down his body in rivers. His muscles were bunching and leaping and coiling, pumped from the enormous exertion. She snapped pictures until there was no more film, until his effort became her exhaustion. She began to feel like her strength was seeping out of her, this experience had been so intense.

And then, in a moment that seemed almost anticlimactic, the calf slipped from his mother's body.

Despite Slim's words, she had allowed herself to hope. But it was obvious the calf was dead, an unearthly stillness upon it. He was reddish brown and white, his fur curly and wet.

But Ty was not giving up. He motioned to Slim who raced to the back of the truck, came back with a handful of grass.

Grass! It didn't seem possible that could help!

Ty took a piece, she saw now it was straw, leaned over and inserted it in the calf's nose and blew.

Nothing.

He blew again, and the calf sneezed! She was so startled she started to laugh. Ty's face brightened. He blew again, and yipped when the calf's stomach rose as it filled with air.

The yip of a warrior who had won against incredible odds.

Looking at him, she knew why he did this. This was one of the only remaining lifestyles in the world that would allow a man like Ty to be who he was—stronger than the strong, fully and completely masculine. This was the world that would test his strength over and over with challenges he would win and lose, too.

She wondered what he did with his heart when he lost.

And then he looked at her and smiled. It was an ageless smile. This time. This time he had won.

He got up, found his shirt, wiped himself down with it,

then pulled it on but left it open. He was exhausted, his shoulders bowed from physical exertion and weariness.

"You think he's going to make it, Slim?"

"I doubt it," Slim said, but he was smiling, too.

With one last effort he gathered the calf in his arms, deposited him at his mother's exhausted nose. She sniffed him and licked him.

"Not many of these guys make it," Ty told her gently. "Maybe one in a thousand."

"But he's going to?"

"I think he just might."

She felt as if she had glimpsed something about him that the world would never see, no matter how many pictures she took. A presence.

A kind of inner strength that matched his outer strength.

"Slim, let's put him in the back of the truck and take him up to the barn. I think Mama will just follow along. Drive slow, not like you normally do."

Under the heifer's watchful eye he picked up the calf again and put him in the back of the truck, then leaped up and sat beside him. Basil inched his head over Ty's arm and regarded the calf with the same loving curiosity he had bestowed on the kittens.

She scrambled up and sat on the other side of the calf. The world seemed magic. But she didn't know if it was because of the little red and white miracle between them, or if it was because of the other miracle between herself and Ty.

Something unfolding in the air.

"You think city girls are going to like those kind of pictures?" he asked, stroking the calf's little head and ears.

She shrugged and realized she was not sure she wanted

to share those pictures with anyone, they were so deeply personal, showed so much of him.

Women would be stampeding to his door if she showed everything she knew about him. She realized she didn't want to share him.

Share him?

That would imply he was hers. And that was a long way from the truth.

Though that had felt like the truth when their lips had touched in the barn. It had felt like she was his and he was hers and that they belonged together.

She realized she was still caught in the power of that force.

And she knew, with surprising clarity, exactly where she wanted it to go. As far as it could go.

She was shocked, and just a little pleased, that she had that kind of girl in her.

"What are you smiling about?" he asked.

"Oh, the calf," she lied.

"Supper is probably ready at the bunkhouse. I can grab a shower there, too. Are you hungry?"

"Actually, if you could drop me off at the house, I need to do some things."

Did he actually look disappointed? She'd make it up to him.

He rapped on the window, and Slim slowed at the house and they let her out. Basil, momentarily torn between her and his newfound love for the calf, chose her. She went in and put away her camera stuff and then looked around.

She was creating a set again, but this time the set was for the seduction of Ty Jordan. And there seemed to be relatively little to work with.

Still, by snooping around just a little she found a nice

tablecloth and some candles. There was a bottle of wine way back in one of the cupboards and there were wine-glasses. She looked through the music he kept by the stereo. Very limited.

Then she went to her own room and looked through her suitcase.

This was so far from what she had planned that she was beginning to doubt she could pull it off.

Then she remembered this had been Stacey's room.

And sure enough the drawers yielded all kinds of little treasures. Scented candles and perfumes. In the cupboard was a long dress. Was that going too far?

Somehow it didn't feel like it.

Stacey had CDs, too. Lots of them. She took one out and put it on the stereo. And then she draped herself on the sofa and waited. And waited. And waited.

And then she fell asleep.

She awoke with a start. The room had grown dark, and she heard Ty on the back step. He came in and turned on the light, froze when he saw her trying to sit up on the couch.

She got up and came to him, took his hand.

"You look beautiful," he said awkwardly, "but I just came up to get my stuff. I'm going to stay with the guys for the rest of the time you're here."

She fell back from him, bit her lip, tried not to cry. She was offering him everything, every single thing she was, and he was going to walk away.

He touched her lip. "Harriet, I thought about it. I know being with you would give me the most pleasure I've ever had. Ever. But that's short term. And I had to ask myself about the long term. What would be best for you and me in the long term. And it's not an affair. You aren't that kind of girl."

"How do you know what kind of girl I am?" she managed to choke out.

He touched her cheek. His hands were rough and leathery, and she rubbed her cheek against the palm.

"I've always known what kind of girl you were," he said.

"And what kind is that?"

"The kind who can make me laugh."

"But not the kind you can love?"

"Harriet, that's the whole problem. I can't love anybody. It's too hard, and it hurts too much."

She thought about the man she'd seen this afternoon. It seemed as if nothing could be too hard for him, it seemed as if he could have no fear.

She felt foolish that she'd introduced the word *love* into the conversation, because she had really and truly convinced herself that was not what it was about for her.

It was going to be about being alive, taking what life offered with both hands, living today, damn the consequences for tomorrow.

But he had seen the truth before she had, and she recognized that.

She just was not that kind of girl. He was right, she would have paid too high a price for a temporary pleasure.

But somehow she didn't feel like thanking him.

At all.

In fact, fury, hard and cold, welled up within her. Before she even knew what she had done, she reached up and smacked his handsome face as hard as she could. It turned his head, and then very slowly he turned back to her, met her eyes without flinching.

She spun on her heel and walked into the bedroom, flung herself on the bed and cried.

Chapter Seven

His duffel bag over his shoulder, Ty knocked on the bunkhouse door. Slim came to the window and peered out at him, then came and opened the door a crack.

"Yeah?" This was said suspiciously, as if Ty didn't drop down here four nights out of five for a cup of coffee or a hand of cards.

"I'm going to spend the night down here."

The door swung open marginally wider, but instead of stepping back and inviting Ty in, Slim crossed his arms and regarded his boss solidly.

"Lovers' quarrel?"

"No," Ty said shortly. "We're not lovers. We're not even friends! We did not quarrel." Ty felt like the handprint was blinking on and off on his cheek. If they hadn't quarreled why was Harriet in Stacey's old room crying?

Slim apparently was not convinced, for he didn't budge, holding out for more details.

With a sigh Ty said, "It just isn't a very good idea for, uh, Harriet and me to be under the same roof right now."

"Why not?" This from Cookie in the background.

"Do you think I could come in? It's cold out here." Every bit of warm clothing that he owned was still in the barn. When Slim looked as if he was going to ignore the request, Ty pushed the door open and stepped in, set down his duffel bag on the rough wooden floor.

He found himself being regarded by three pairs of sullen eyes.

"What?"

"Well, me and the guys were just talking about this," Slim said.

"About what?" Ty asked. His body hurt from pulling that calf. His head hurt from trying to figure out that confounded woman.

And his heart hurt because of the look on her face when she had smacked him. He looked longingly at the empty bunk across the room. That's all he wanted. To put his head down, pull a pillow over his eyes and be blessed with the oblivion of sleep.

"About you and Harriet," Pete said.

Oh-oh. This had to be headed off at the pass. "There is no me and Harriet. She's here to do a job. I'm doing my damnedest to survive it."

"Well, we don't quite see it that way."

"Really?" Ty asked, inserting a very cold note into his voice.

Slim was undeterred. "We figure you hide out here on the ranch like a hermit, so God brought a woman to you. You know, since you weren't goin' lookin' for one."

Ty's desire to laugh was stifled by the solemn looks on the three faces. Cookie was nodding his head sagely, as if he had a personal pipeline to God.

"I didn't realize you three old reprobates had found religion," Ty said.

"That just goes to show, you don't know us old 'reprobates' as well as you might think," Slim said, putting just enough emphasis on reprobate to let Ty know he knew what the word meant and he was offended it had been used to describe him.

"Look, if I can just lie down the night here without the lecture—"

"Nope," Slim said.

"Pardon?"

"You heard me."

"I can't lie down? Or I have to have the lecture before I lie down?" It occurred to him the fact that he was negotiating was ludicrous. Though it was an item that didn't get brought up much, the simple truth of the matter was he was the boss. "Are you conveniently forgetting I own the place?"

"Well, fire me, then," Slim said.

"Us," Cookie and Pete joined in. They stood up and ambled over, slouched, thumbs hooked in the belt loops on their jeans, looking defiant. They also looked big and menacing, like outlaws in a bad Western.

"You got a chance not to end up like this, boss," Cookie said slowly. "Alone, lonely, playing cards at night."

"We like playing cards!" Ty reminded them somewhat desperately. He looked at the resolute, seamed faces of men who had been his friends and family for as long as he could remember. He'd never thought of these guys as alone or lonely. They had seemed perfectly content. But Cookie's words were an eerie echo of thoughts he'd been having himself lately.

"You could get yourself a wife," Pete said. "I like the idea of little cowpunchers running around on the place."

"You don't just get yourself a wife as if it's mail-order or something," Ty sputtered. He didn't even want his mind to start going to how the little cowpunchers arrived. "It's more complicated than that."

His three ranch hands stood there, as unmovable as rocks, as if they thought he was going to go over the complications with them now.

"Could we talk about this in the morning? Please?" Ty said. "I'm done in."

"Sure," Slim said, and then as if he'd given a secret signal, all three men converged on Ty. They were unbelievably strong, and of course he wasn't expecting what happened next. Cookie and Pete each grabbed a leg and hefted him up. Slim slipped behind him and encircled his chest with his arms. And then they threw him bodily out the door.

Ty landed hard, and muscles already aching from his struggle with the calf cried out in protest. His duffel bag landed in the dirt by his head, and the door shut firmly behind him. He heard the bolt click shut, the gleeful cackling of the men behind the door.

He lay there for a moment, contemplating this ugly new development in his life. But the cold forced him to move on. Ty stood up slowly, brushed himself off and glared at the door. Then he shivered. He sure as hell wasn't going to beg them, foolish old men. Matchmakers. He was never going to let them hear the end of this, how they had stooped so low as to start minding another man's business.

Ty shouldered his bag and headed back up to the house. With any luck, she'd be in bed by now, done crying, and he could creep into his own bedroom, unnoticed, and go to sleep.

Sure enough, the house was in complete darkness. He actually felt a moment's gratitude that he no longer had a screen door on the back, since it had squeaked outrageously. But when he went to open the back door, the knob clicked under his hand but did not turn.

It took him a moment to get it.

She had locked the door! Harriet Pendleton had locked him out of his own house. Had she known he would come back? He could still feel the sting of her hand on his cheek. Still, he doubted she had locked him out on purpose.

No, she was a city girl, used to locking doors at night. It was probably second nature to her, like brushing her teeth.

He regarded his door with a scowl. He tried to remember if it had ever been locked before. He was pretty sure it hadn't been. He didn't even know if a key existed.

He heard a noise and looked up hopefully at the kitchen window. It would be embarrassing if it was Harriet, but he was damn near frozen, so his pride was going to have to take the kicking.

But it wasn't Harriet.

It was the damned dog, his nose pressed up against the kitchen window. In order for that dog to be looking out the window, he had to be on the counter. He was probably helping himself to the loaf of bread that was there, plastic and all.

The mean facts were the dog was in his house and Ty was out. His loyal staff had thrown him off his own property, showing him about as much respect as a bouncer would show a drunk at the local bar.

Feeling his temper rising at the unfairness of life, Ty considered kicking down the door. But then he'd probably scare Harriet. And then she might need comforting. And then they'd be right back at the place that had got him slapped in the first place. She needed things he couldn't give her.

He remembered he had two perfectly warm jackets in the barn. Sighing, he shouldered the duffel bag once more and headed down there. He checked the calf, who was still very much alive, looking bright and vigorous, his mother content beside him. His coats were in the loft where he had left them.

Pulling on the big wool one, he burrowed into the hay and tried to sleep. Hay poked him. The kittens, lively at night, came out and scampered around him and over him. It was cold in here despite the jacket. He wrapped his other jacket around his legs, burrowed deeper into the hay. Ty had always imagined that hell would be hot, but he knew beyond a shadow of a doubt he was in hell right now, and it was cold.

In bits and snatches he snoozed. His dreams were peppered with restless thoughts and disturbing images, many of them having to do with the fullness of Harriet Pendleton's bottom lip. A man had never been happier to see the morning light coming through the slats of the barn.

He'd bypass her this morning. Surely the guys wouldn't refuse him breakfast?

As he came to the bunkhouse, he could hear laughter inside. Including hers. Well, what was he supposed to do? They had to work together. He couldn't avoid her forever.

He shoved open the bunkhouse door, and the laughter ceased as if the laugh track on a sitcom had broken down.

All eyes, none of them inviting, were on him.

"'Morning," he said. The dog was under the table. Even Basil ignored him, snuffling happily for scraps.

"Good morning, Ty." It was she who answered, her voice all brisk and businesslike. She was wearing a very unattractive pair of khaki pants and something that looked like a flak jacket. She had little dark circles under her eyes and looked as if she might have been crying.

Which explained the looks he was getting from the guys—murderous.

"Pete and Slim and Cookie were just having a look at my storyboards." Harriet told him, and they all leaned back over the table, generals planning an attack, and ignored him.

Ty bit back the comment that his guys wouldn't know a storyboard from a Gucci bag, but they all did appear to know what a storyboard was.

"We were talking about the summer shots," she said sweetly, "and they came up with the most wonderful suggestion."

Were his men smirking? Exchanging crafty smiles and sidelong glances loaded with malicious mirth? No doubt about it.

"They said there's a pond on the property, a swimming hole, complete with a tire swing. Wouldn't that make a terrific July shot?"

"Terrific, except for the fact the ice has been off that pond for about a week. It would be cold enough to freeze the—"

Slim gave him a cautioning look. Come on! She'd been in war zones. She knew all about brass monkeys!

Still, he changed direction. "—the spots off old Basil here."

"You don't actually have to go in the water," she explained with elaborate patience. "Just make it look like you're going to go in. Swing around on the tire a bit."

"That sounds like fun," he said, with not one ounce of sincerity. He shot her conspirators a look. "Thanks, guys."

"'Welcome," Slim said happily. "We're gonna come watch."

What was this? A complete revolution? Nobody

worked on this ranch anymore? Nobody consulted him about what they were doing for the day?

Apparently not. They were all poring over her storyboard.

"You know, for the fall picture," Cookie said, "we could stage a roundup scene. Branding fires, roping. I could maybe be in the background at the chuck wagon. For authenticity."

"Really?" she breathed, as if having Cookie in the background stirring a big steaming pot of beans would make her every dream come true.

"Do you think I could be in the background, too?" Slim asked shyly.

"Of course," she said. "You, too, Pete."

Ty glared at them all. "This is day five," he reminded them. "A roundup scene would take a while to set up. We don't want Harriet to be behind schedule."

"Actually, I'm ahead of schedule," she told him coolly. "Two more days should wrap it up. I could be gone by tomorrow night, if I can figure out the winter scenes."

Cookie slapped a plate on the table for him.

The eggs were scrambled, which Ty hated, and the bacon wasn't crisp. And he saw today would not be a good day to register a complaint. Tomorrow night? That was great. Why didn't he feel great? Because the bacon was damned near raw, that's why.

"Winter!" Slim said. "There's still snow up the mountains. We could—"

"—run a ranch?" Ty cut him off, hopefully.

"—go up there," Slim said, as if Ty had not spoken. "Snow will be real soft at this time of year. Look."

Slim had gotten the storyboard idea, and he quickly

sketched a snowman with a man behind it ducking from snowballs.

"You could use the dog, too," he went on enthusiastically. "Them kind of dogs were used in the snow for rescues. I wonder if we have something we could put around his neck!" He added the dog to his sketch.

"I could make a little barrel out of that pickled herring container!" Cookie crowed.

Ty felt the headache, which had never quite disappeared, leap back into the foreground.

"That would be so perfect," Harriet said, as if she was completely unaware that she was breaking all the rules. "We could do the roundup scene in the morning, snow in the afternoon, and by evening I'm out of here."

"You don't have to rush off," Pete said sulkily. "We're just gettin' to know you."

Ty knew it was his duty to remind her of the rules, even if it was going to make him the most unpopular guy on the ranch. "My life's not supposed to be disrupted, remember? I'm hardly supposed to know you're here, remember?"

His men looked as if they were considering tossing him out again.

"Don't be such a stick-in-the-mud," Slim told him mildly, and went back to sketching. "Look, we could—"

"If we play by the rules," she said quietly, "I probably won't be able to get away tomorrow night."

Ty couldn't even listen anymore. He stuffed back the food in record time. "I guess I'll go check the cows and do the chores," he said, a definite hint.

"Great," Pete agreed, not jumping out of his chair and offering to come help at all. "The sun won't be high enough for the swimming hole picture for a while anyway. What kind of swim trunks you got, boss?''

Unless Stacey was around, Ty generally swam naked.

"I got a pair of cutoff jeans," he said curtly.

Pete looked disappointed. ''One of those Speedo things like they wear at the swim competitions would be better, huh, Harriet?''

"Oh, much better," she said, straight-faced. She was enjoying tormenting him! This was her revenge for being scorned last night.

"I could go to town and try and find one," Pete said seriously.

"No!" Ty said through clenched teeth. "No, as in not if my life depended on it. No, as in never. No, as in not until hell freezes over." Which, he knew firsthand, it had done last night.

Pete and Harriet broke up laughing, and Ty looked from one to the other and got to his feet with all the dignity he could manage. He went to the door and out into the bright sunshine. A perfect damned day to shoot summer pictures. He suspected his prayers for rain were going to go unanswered, now that those old reprobates had decided to bend God's ear.

Still, if he thought Harriet had been enjoying her revenge at the bunkhouse, it was nothing compared to the opportunity she had several hours later as Ty stood shivering beside the tire swing that was suspended over Jordan's Pond.

A wind had picked up from the north, and though the day looked bright and beautiful, as was so typical of Alberta at this time of year, the cold was absolutely stinging.

And Ty was in nothing but a pair of cutoff jeans. They had started out just above his knee but the evil elf helpers had decided they would sexier shorter and had sawed off the legs to his thighs with their pocketknives.

When he'd protested, he'd been reminded sternly, that it was for a good cause, and then Pete had nicked him with the knife, so he had decided he better just keep his mouth shut.

Still, the fashion adjustment had left a lot more bare flesh exposed to the bite of that north wind.

Harriet's entourage was thoroughly enjoying his discomfort.

"That shade of blue around your lips ain't going to look good in the picture, boss!"

"Come on, go for a dip. It would make a great picture."

"Quit shiverin'. You'll blur the pictures."

But Ty noticed, without satisfaction, that she didn't seem to be as tickled with his discomfort as the guys.

"It's too cold for this today," she decided. She pulled her own jacket tighter around her. "Ty, let's forget it."

"Let's just get on with it." Proving oneself tough as nails must be right up there with male preening, because he couldn't seem to bring himself to duck out of this. Of course, he told himself, ducking out today just meant one more day of picture taking tacked on somewhere else.

"Well, if you're sure," she said doubtfully, "get on the tire."

The tire was suspended from a thick branch of a maple that leaned way out over the water. He climbed out onto the branch, then shinnied along it to the rope. He lowered himself down onto the tire. So far, so good. Not a drop of water on him. He began to pump to get it swinging over the water.

Basil, who seemed to have joined the Merry Men permanently, went nuts, running up and down the shore of the pond, barking hysterically each time the tire spun out over the water.

"Boss, smile!"

Ty bared his teeth. More evidence of hell freezing over. He was not sure when he had ever been so cold. Without being asked, he struck several different poses on the swinging tire. He sat on top of it, square on. He put his legs through the hole, and rode it like a swing. He was so cold he felt like a wooden puppet. If the goose bumps got any bigger they were going to show up in the photographs!

Apparently, from the discontented mutterings of the guys on shore, they were not too impressed with his smile or his poses. Harriet, only her mouth visible from behind the camera, was frowning.

"Look happy," Cookie called helpfully over the distressed woofs of the dog.

"You come out here and try looking happy," he called back through chattering teeth.

"Okay," Harriet called. "Enough. It's not warm enough for this. The poor man will catch his death. Ty come on in. We can try this a different day."

A different day? That meant extending her visit. That meant his life turned topsy-turvy for more time. *The poor man* almost made it sound as if he might be forgiven for last night. Obviously, this was no time to quit! He tried harder to look happy. He pumped the tire until it was swinging in a wild arc over the pond, and then climbed out on the edge of it, straddled it and rode it bucking horse style.

"Ride 'em, cowboy," Pete yelled with enthusiasm.

"That's more like it," Cookie agreed.

"You're going to fall off," Harriet called, this funny little edge of panic in her voice. "Ty, don't do that."

Of course, then he had to do it one-handed.

"I wish you wouldn't," she said weakly, but she was snapping pictures like crazy, which meant maybe they wouldn't have to come back here a different day, after all.

Ty scrambled up, until he was standing on top of the tire again. He held the rope with both hands and propelled the tire outward with his legs. The rope acted like a bungee, throwing the tire up and down.

Basil howled his disapproval of such antics.

"Okay," Harriet said nervously, as if he was perched over a thousand sharpened swords. "That's it. I've got everything I need. Come on in."

"Hey, cannonball into the water!" Pete yelled with sudden and enthusiastic inspiration. "That would make a great summer picture!"

"Yeah, boss, jump."

"Come on, it would make a great picture!" Slim joined in.

He scowled at his employees. They were forgetting how easy it was going to be for him to get even, to exact revenge. The next time there was a blizzard all three of them were going to be riding fences, including Cookie, who hadn't been on a horse in a lot of years.

"Jump!" Pete yelled.

"Don't you dare," Harriet called. "Don't be ridiculous. It's much too cold for that. Steer the tire over here. Can you climb back up the rope onto the branch?"

"Don't you dare?" He studied her as the tire swooped by her. Her great big eyes were anxious. She really didn't want him to jump into the water. Even he could see what a great photo it would make.

"Get off of there," she said.

She was getting a little mad.

What did that mean, that she was putting his welfare ahead of the stupid picture? That she was worried about him? Considering the events of last night, that would not be a good thing. At all. So why did he feel kind of good about the distressed expression on her face?

"Ty, would you get down from there before you catch your death?" she pleaded.

"Come on, boss, jump!"

"You guys stop it!" she said sternly.

But the evil elves were in full rebellion now. "Jump! Jump!"

Ty pumped the tire out higher over the water. He noticed her reluctance as she put the camera up to her eye and took more pictures. But between every shot she yelled at him to come in.

Quite a bit of chaos in there on shore, with her yelling for him to come in and the guys yelling for him to jump and the dog barking frantically.

It was actually quite fun being right where he was. He didn't even feel cold anymore. He planted his feet side by side on the narrow rim of the tire, held on to the rope with one hand and leaned way out over the water.

"Stop it!" she squealed.

"Jump!" the guys yelled.

He laughed out loud. He pumped the tire higher, threaded his legs through the hole, hard, and leaned back. He hung upside down, letting his fingertips trail in the water.

When he pulled himself upright, she was looking pale and worried. It had been a long, long time since anybody worried about him. That was his job, to worry. About Stacey. About cattle. About bills. Even about those three old reprobates working themselves into a frenzy on shore.

"Ty, please," she called. "I'll never forgive myself if you get sick from this."

"It would take a lot more than a little water to make him sick," Cookie yelled. "Get wet, boss. It'll sell a zillion calendars."

"A zillion, eh?" He pulled himself back up on top of the tire.

"Two zillion!" Pete called.

"I'll buy one myself," Slim yelled.

"Stop it, you three," she commanded. "Stop it this instant! He'll catch pneumonia. He'll get hypothermia!"

Ty considered the possibilities. "Cannonball or somersault?" he asked.

"Do a cannonball first," Pete yelled. "Then a somersault."

That was pushing it. He was going into that water once, and once only.

"Neither," she was screaming. "Ty Jordan. You get down from there."

"Yes, ma'am," he said pleasantly. Obviously a somersault would make a better picture. Much more spectacular. But harder to catch his face, and not as dramatic a splash.

"Get the camera ready!" Slim said. "He's gonna do it!"

"I'll never speak to you again," Harriet said, but she was getting the camera ready.

"Promises, promises," he called back. He launched himself, stretching high toward the sun, and then he folded, grabbed his knees and hit the water.

Nothing could have prepared him for the cold. His limbs went instantly numb. Still, the shore was only feet away, and he could have made it easily, except that Basil, bellowing frantically, plunged into the water, bent on rescuing Ty.

The huge dog had only paddled a few awkward strokes when apparently it occurred to him he could not swim. His red-rimmed eyes panicked, he glanced at shore, then toward Ty. His gaze locked on Ty, and he launched himself forward.

It was like being hit with three hundred pounds of soaking-wet mop. The wet fur had made the dog nearly double in weight, and Ty went under, felt the ice-cold water rushing into his mouth and up his nose. He shoved hard on the dog and got free of him, but Basil rushed right back at him, clawing the water, until his paws found shoulders. He shoved Ty under again.

Ty came up coughing, Basil put both his paws on his head and tried to climb up his body. This time, when he went under, Ty dove away from the dog, surfaced a few feet from him. The dog spotted him and headed toward him. Man and dog raced for shore. Ty hit it first, but just barely. He crawled out and lay there gasping. Basil pulled himself out right behind him, and lay down beside him, a huge heap of smelly, wet, contrite dog.

He licked Ty's face. Ty felt stupidly happy that the dog had not drowned himself. "Dumb mutt," he said, and gave the dog a quick scratch behind the ears.

Then he managed to pull himself to his feet, to face Harriet's fury.

"You idiot. You could have drowned. Get him a blanket," she snapped to her motley lieutenants, then turned to him. "How could you do something so ridiculous? Someone get the truck running. Ty, get in that truck cab."

"You promised you weren't speaking to me," he reminded her mildly as Slim handed him an old blanket that had seen the back of many horses. He unfolded it and tossed it around his shoulders. "I didn't figure on Basil coming in."

"You could have been killed."

"And a damned poor way it would have been to die," he said, trying to make it into a joke. Apparently he failed utterly.

Harriet started to cry. Just like that.

Suddenly her noisy assistants were incredibly silent. Cookie was looking out over the water. Pete was investigating something under his thumbnail, and Slim had taken a sudden and passionate interest in the toe of his boot.

"We were just funning," Slim said uneasily after a full minute of looking at his boot. Then he grabbed the dog by the collar, and Pete and Cookie joined him in the race for the truck cab.

Cookie hit him on the shoulder, hard, on the way by. "Do something," he hissed.

Ty glared at their retreating backs. "Hey, don't put that dog in the cab wet! I'll never get the smell—"

The door slammed, Basil inside. So much for being boss.

Finally Ty looked at her. She wouldn't look at him. No wonder those guys had run for their lives. Nothing made a man go softer than a woman in tears. Nothing.

He sighed and took a step toward her. She still wouldn't look at him. He sighed again and opened the blanket around his shoulders so it included her. Then he folded her back in against his chest.

Homecoming. Having her pressed against him felt like coming home.

"It wasn't really dangerous," he said. "Just cold. Uncomfortable. See? I'm not even shaking." She was shaking more than him, though he decided not to point that out.

He should have known being rational was not going to help.

She thumped her fist soundly against his chest. "The dog nearly killed you."

He chuckled. "Basil did seem to overestimate his rescue abilities. He'll probably be drummed out of the rescue-dog corps."

"How can you laugh about it?" He felt her tears trickle down his naked chest. They were pleasantly warm. And then she took a deep breath and took a quick step back. "Go get in the truck before you freeze to death."

And then she looked at him. Directly into his eyes. Her eyes were moist and a beautiful, soft brown, like suede.

And what he saw in her eyes nearly stopped his heart far more than the jolt of the cold water had.

The woman loved him.

And that was far more dangerous than her just wanting him, and far more dangerous than the monster weight of that dog pulling him under the water.

Ty felt a warmth spreading through his face and then his legs and then his chest. It was as if he stood in the light of a ten-foot-high bonfire, instead of outside, soaking wet, in the icy Alberta wind.

Chapter Eight

Ty was shivering and shaking on the seat of the truck, sandwiched in between Slim who was driving and Harriet. The cab, a crew cab, large enough for all of them, smelled of wet dog and cigar smoke and horse blankets. Cookie had guiltily extinguished a big, black stogie when Harriet and Ty had gotten into the truck.

The heater was going full blast, and Harriet pressed her forehead against the window and tried to convince herself it was the smell of the dog and the cigar and the heat blasting out of the vents that was making her feel sick.

But in her heart she knew it wasn't. It was the tension of watching Ty nearly drown that was making her stomach so queasy. More than that, it was the look she had seen on Ty's face moments ago when they stood at the water's edge, his arms around her.

He knew.

She had seen the light of understanding come on in the liquid darkness of his eyes. He knew her deepest secret, the secret she had managed to keep even from herself.

Her mission. Harriet had told herself it was about getting her power back. About overcoming a childish infatuation that she should have outgrown years ago.

Now she saw it in more simple terms. Harriet Pendleton had come back to the Bar ZZ for the express purpose of falling out of love with Ty Jordan. In that respect her mission was a complete failure.

More than a failure.

A complete and utter fiasco.

"You're sure gettin' some great pictures," Slim said with satisfaction. The road they were on was little more than a wagon track, and each bump they hit did more damage to her stomach. "I'm looking forward to seeing the swimming hole ones."

Well, maybe her mission wasn't a complete disaster. Harriet knew she was taking the best photographs she had ever taken. She knew all those secret feelings she harbored for Ty would lend to the finished photos. The pictures would have a depth of emotion, a shine, that could not be fabricated. The pictures would capture his essence in a way only a woman who loved him could capture his essence.

Desperately searching for a bright spot, Harriet decided maybe being in love with him had a good side. The better those photographs turned out, the more calendars that would sell. She was being of service. Her pain served a greater purpose. If she looked at it that way, she should be able to keep her sanity for just one and a half more days.

Of course, the first job was going to be to convince Ty he had been mistaken about what he had seen bald and unvarnished in her face at the edge of the swimming hole. She had thought he was going to die—and that it was going to be her fault. For bringing Basil in the first place, for agreeing to the swimming hole shots when she had known it was too cold.

Lady Disaster.

But when Ty had survived, nothing could have kept her joy, her relief and, yes, her love, from her face. Now she had to find a way to erase that unguarded moment from his memory bank.

He shivered violently beside her, and she risked a glance at him. His flawless skin was pebbled with goose bumps. He was a little blue around his lips.

All that love surged forward again!

"Ty needs to get to a hot shower," she said, and realized her error immediately when Pete and Slim and Cookie all snickered. If she was going to convince everybody that she was not the least bit in love with Ty Jordan, especially him, she couldn't continue to entertain these tough men by being a mother hen. "I can't have him getting sick," she said, stripping the emotion from her voice. "It would wreck my shooting schedule."

She actually felt the arrow find its mark. Ty flinched beside her, and she felt the dark intensity of his gaze rest on her face.

"Thanks for your heartfelt concern," he drawled sarcastically.

The perfect reaction. Harriet refused to look at him.

"It would take more than a little water to make him sick," Pete assured her. "He hasn't always been a fragile male model."

That cracked them up completely. She cast Ty a look. His face had the set of granite to it. Slim pulled the truck up in front of Ty's house, and she opened the truck door. The bouncing, the heat, and the smells had taken their toll. She rushed behind the truck and was sick.

She felt a hand stroking the back of her neck, strong,

soothing, amazingly gentle. It probably said something about the state of her love life, that she found the moment almost heartbreakingly tender.

"Are you okay?" he asked.

"It's the cigar smoke," she said. "Go get that shower. I'm okay."

His hand lingered on her neck for a moment and then dropped to his side. "Go with the guys," he said. "Cookie will take care of you."

She wanted it to be Ty taking care of her, so she wouldn't even look at him, just in case that latest weakness was written in neon across her face.

Basil had evidently decided he owed his life to Ty because he shambled down the walk after him. The guys called out wardrobe suggestions, laughing when Ty slammed the door on them.

Well, what did she expect? Ty Jordan was irresistible to man and beast. And woman. And that was going to sell calendars by the ton, she reminded herself.

When they arrived at the bunkhouse, Cookie hustled her inside and sat her down at the rough table. In moments he put a large glass of some sort of potion in front of her that bubbled and smoked and foamed.

"Drink every drop," he said.

She did, and was amazed by how well she felt by the time Ty showed up at the bunkhouse half an hour later. She noticed he had ignored the wardrobe instructions. Then again, it really didn't matter what he wore.

His jeans had the knee out of them, and the denim shirt was faded nearly white. It was far sexier than anything he could have put on in an attempt to be that.

And it was apparent he'd also had enough of being bossed around by his staff.

"Pete, Slim," he called. "Let's go. We got work to

do.'' The tone brooked absolutely no argument. He had completely recuperated from the shivering wreck he'd been half an hour ago. He looked vital and strong, and she knew he was one of those men who was just pure steel, toughness at his very core.

But then she remembered the tenderness of his hand on the back of her neck and wondered if it really was toughness at his core.

The men exchanged glances. It was evident to everyone Ty's good humor was at an end. When Harrict got up, too, he frowned.

''Not you.''

She felt her cheeks burn. Her affections had been so embarrassingly apparent he didn't even want to be around her anymore. Well, who could blame him?

''Get over that tummy ache,'' he ordered, softening the blow. ''We're going to be doing some hard riding. We're behind on everything. I can't slow up for you right now. Especially not,'' he glowered at his men, ''if we're doing that roundup scene tomorrow.''

He turned on his heel and walked out, Pete and Slim, subdued, cast her an apologetic glance and then tailed behind him.

''Ain't he the crabby one?'' Cookie said cheerfully. ''You know how to make cookies? My chocolate chip recipe won a ribbon at the fair a few years back.''

Harriet wasn't sure which question to respond to. ''He does seem a little crabby,'' she ventured, ''and I'll take the blame. That was an awful lot to ask of him. He should never have gone in the water.''

''Nonsense. It's good for him. It's good for all of us. We get in a rut around here.''

''Well, from the look on his face he might disagree about how good it was for him.'' She was eager to get off the topic. "And, no, I don't know how to make cookies."

"Well, I do. That's where the name comes from. And an hour from now, you'll know how, too."

She hoped there was no ulterior motive here. The guys thinking a woman for Ty would have to know how to cook, look after him. They were very traditional men. And they probably expected a certain amount of tradition from their women.

That thought should cheer her. In order to fit in here on the Bar ZZ, she probably would have to wear an apron, cook things, sew on buttons, knit sweaters. And in that case she would never fit in. See? It was a blessing that Ty had scorned her every advance. He could probably tell by looking at her all the things she was about to confess to Cookie.

"I'm not domestic," she said, with a certain proud defiance. "I tend to microwave at home. Lean Cuisine."

Cookie gave her a baffled look, as if she was speaking a foreign language. She realized she had to make it more simple.

"Cookie, I've never baked a cake or cooked a turkey. I suppose a woman on a ranch is probably expected to be able to feed the crew. Make bread and pies and roast beef and all that kind of stuff." It exhausted her thinking about it.

"Not on this ranch," Cookie said with a scowl. "What would I do?"

"Well, while we're on the subject, there's lots of other things I can't do. I can't be trusted with laundry. White turns to pink, and sweaters shrink. I also cannot be trusted with bleach. And babies are iffy, as well."

"What are you tellin' me for?" Cookie asked, distressed.

"Just in case you guys had notions. About me and Ty." She felt foolish as soon as she said it. Anybody with eyes could tell she and Ty were in different leagues entirely.

"Don't care if you can bake a cake. And I'm a little iffy in the baby department myself. They scare the hell out of me, frankly."

"Me, too," she breathed, astounded by this unexpected discovery of a kindred spirit.

"The boy's dying of loneliness," Cookie confided in her. "If cakes and clean shirts had a hope of fixing that, it would be fixed already." Cookie put a bowl in front of her that looked big enough to take a swim in.

Did Cookie and the boys think she was the antidote to Ty's loneliness? Were they doing a bit of plotting? It would be funny if it wasn't so scary.

"He is not dying of loneliness," she said firmly. "I have rarely seen a man so content in his own competency. He doesn't need anyone."

"That's sure as hell what he wants to believe. Got you fooled, too, I see." Cookie shook his head mournfully.

"I'm not fooled. It's just that he is not interested in me in a way that would solve his loneliness problems, presuming he had them." She realized her error of omission, and added hastily, "Not that I'm interested in him in that way, either."

"Humph."

She had obviously failed to convince Cookie. She looked with horror at the stained recipe that Cookie was flattening out with his palm in front of her. "Twelve cups of flour? Are you joking?"

"No sense making a dinky batch for this crew. The boy has feelings for you. Written all over him. You think he jumped in that water to impress me?"

"He did it because he's a rebel. He doesn't have feelings for me,'' Harriet said firmly, carefully measuring out the first of the flour. She was not going to let this old man fan to life the very hope inside her that she was trying to extinguish. "Except maybe aversion. He might feel aversion for me."

"Aversion? What's that mean?"

"He doesn't like me," Harriet said. It was good to say the words, to stab herself with them, to feel the pain. She looked at the next ingredient on her list. It seemed to be swimming in front of her eyes.

"Oh, you're reading it all wrong," Cookie said, and he wasn't talking about the recipe. "If he has aversion, it ain't for you. He's managed to come through a whole lot of years without feeling nothin' at all. I bet you're shakin' up his nice safe world something fierce."

Obviously, Ty Jordan's world was not the least bit safe. He rode horses and wrestled cattle and battled blizzards. He did dangerous things, day in and day out, but she knew better than to point that out to Cookie, who would scorn the things she thought were dangerous. City girl, the gap between her and Ty widening by the second.

Given that the situation was hopeless, romantically speaking, Harriet begged herself not to take advantage of this wonderful opportunity to spy into Ty's personal life. But she was like a junkie being offered a fix. Cookie wanted to talk about him, and she wanted to hear.

"How come he doesn't feel anything?" she asked casually, squinting at the recipe as if she was trying to fuse atoms.

"He was just a kid when his folks died. It gave him all the wrong ideas about caring about people. Love hurt him, and it hurt him bad. He don't want to feel that again."

She shoveled sugar into the cookies. "You don't have

to worry about him loving me. I know I don't have a chance.''

''Really? Why's that?''

''Oh, Cookie. I don't have any illusions about myself. I'm gangly and stringy and outspoken. I'm not the kind of woman Ty needs.''

''I think you're attractive,'' Cookie said with gruff sincerity. ''You must have hurts as good as his if you don't think so. Because there's other ways of saying gangly and stringy, like tall and willowy.''

They were supposed to be spying on Ty's personal life, not hers!

''I just mean I'm not good enough for him. Cookie, they did that survey at the mall. Every woman who saw his picture loved him. How do I have a chance against that?''

''You saying *you* love him?''

She gasped. Oh, she was revealing far too much of herself. This cagey cooking cowboy had her doing too many things at once! Now she'd forgotten how much baking soda she'd put in. Had she put in baking soda?

''Of course I don't love him,'' she said vehemently. ''I only know he's just about the best-looking man in the world, and that's a little too much for a girl like me.''

Cookie grunted. ''He don't have no idea what he looks like. All this attention about his looks aggravates him. I had a feeling you saw something else in him. Deeper than what his face looks like.''

''Well, I don't,'' she said stubbornly, which probably rated as one of the worst lies she had ever told.

''How much salt you put in there?''

She had no idea. ''Just what the recipe says.''

''Humph. Just for the record you got it all wrong. He

don't feel like he's too good for anyone. More like not good enough.''

"But why?"

"You should ask him that."

It hurt Harriet to think of Ty feeling as if he wasn't good enough. "Maybe I will," she said thoughtfully, and then gave her full attention to the cookies.

It seemed to take her hours to make them. The batch was so big it hurt her arms to stir it. She and Cookie sampled them when they finally came out of his big oven. They were absolutely awful.

Cookie munched thoughtfully. "Too much salt," he decided. "And you mighta forgot the baking soda."

What did he expect? She'd been distracted!

"Let's throw them out," she begged.

But too late. The guys came back in the door and headed right for the cookie sheets. Pete and Slim each grabbed a handful, but of course it was Ty she watched.

Watched him and entertained the most painful of fantasies. Would he come through his door one day to a young wife who had baked him cookies, who was waiting eagerly for his reaction, his approval?

He took a cookie and popped the whole thing in his mouth. His chewing suddenly slowed, he gulped. He looked at Cookie. He stopped chewing altogether and looked at her. Manfully he chewed and swallowed.

"I don't need your damned approval, anyway," she told him. "I'm not that kind of woman."

"Did I say anything?" Ty asked. "What kind of woman?"

She was aware the rest of the men were watching her, as if she was a she-bear trapped in the cabin with them.

"The kind who bakes cookies and knows how to cook turkey." She threw it down like a gauntlet.

Ty shot her a look. "So," he asked cautiously, "what kind of woman are you?"

"Fiercely independent. And tall."

"I kind of figured those out for myself," Ty said.

"And you don't approve?"

"I never said that!"

"Well, do you?"

"I thought you didn't need my damned approval," he reminded her, "but just for the record I like tall just fine. And independent."

The guys were all smiling broadly, as if Ty was successfully negotiating a minefield for all of them.

"Have another cookie," Cookie said deviously.

Pete and Slim were obediently reaching for more cookies!

"Don't," she said proudly. "Please. I know I'm a failure at all things domestic."

What she really felt like was a failure at all things. She shot Ty a look. He was sliding her a little look, too.

Pity. As if he saw her baking cookies as another hopeless effort for her to win him over, even after she'd denied it. A case of thou doth protest too much, obviously. Ty thought if she couldn't win him with kisses, she'd try the more traditional method.

She wasn't going to be pitied by him.

It would be better if he hated her than pitied her.

"We should try a new hairstyle for the shoot tomorrow," she said, narrowing her eyes at him. "Have you ever had mousse in your hair?"

"A moose in my hair? Cookie, what did you give her to settle her stomach?"

The guys all had a good chuckle over that.

"How about an elk? You ever had an elk in your hair, Ty?" Pete asked.

"No, but I had a deer once," Ty said. "Came right through the windshield. I was picking him out of my hair for days."

She wasn't going to be pitied by him, and she wasn't going to be made fun of, either. "Mousse," she said, through gritted teeth. "Hairstyling product."

He pondered her for a moment, then smiled, slow and sweet and sexy. "I think I like the deer better."

"Cookie, how long until supper?" she asked.

"A bit."

"Oh, goodie. Enough time for me to style Ty's hair. Have a seat."

"No," he said, folding his arms over his chest and planting his legs.

"Come on, boss," Slim said. "Fabio probably has his hair styled."

"Who the hell is Fabio?"

"Let her fiddle with your hair," Cookie said, "or I ain't givin' you no dinner."

Ty glared at them all, then, muttering about a conspiracy, took a chair at the table.

And by the time she was done styling his hair, she was halfway to her goal. Ty Jordan didn't pity her at all. He pitied himself.

Only, in a way her plan had backfired. Because nothing could have prepared her for the sheer delight of running her hands through the silk of his earth-dark hair, for the quiver that touching him put in the bottom of her belly.

After a dinner that proved no woman on the Bar ZZ was ever going to have to produce a meal, not while Cookie lived and breathed, Harriet decided she didn't want to even be in the same room as Ty anymore.

The hair, spiked up, looked sinfully sexy. She could

not get the way it had felt beneath her fingertips—springy and clean—out of her mind.

"I'm going to bed," she announced. "Good night, all."

"You want me to walk you up there?"

She had not missed the sharp nudge to the ribs that Ty had taken from Slim before he had made the offer.

"That won't be at all necessary. I can look after myself. Besides, Basil will come with me, won't you?"

The dog got to his feet and they trundled out the door together. She did not allow herself to wonder where Ty was going to spend the night.

Basil accompanied her up to the house. He sneezed three times getting there. By the time they got to the door, she was aware that the swim had obviously done more harm to Basil than Ty. So even though she knew Ty preferred the dog be left outside, she invited him in.

That was a mistake. Once inside the door, the dog made a beeline for Ty's bedroom, nudged open the partially closed door with his nose and then launched himself onto the bed.

"Get off of there," she told him sternly. Her plan might be to make Ty dislike her, but even she knew this was going too far. The dog rolled around happily on the comforter. Inside the small room it was painfully clear he still smelled damp and rank from his swim.

"Get off," she pleaded, tugging on him. She discovered that one hundred and twenty pounds of woman was no match at all for one hundred and fifty pounds of determined dog. Basil settled himself more deeply into the comforter.

"You're lucky Ty probably isn't coming in tonight," she said, but even as she said it, she heard the back door open and shut, his boots hitting the stairs.

Then Ty was standing in the doorway, looking at them both, his arms folded over his chest. His eyes were dark and mysterious and his body was beautiful and she wanted nothing more than to fling herself at him—just like nine out of every ten women who saw him.

And she fully intended to have some pride. The new game plan, she reminded herself, was to make him dislike her instead of pity her.

"What's that dog doing in my bed?"

"Oh," she said sweetly. "I put him there. He has a terrible cold. Don't you baby?"

For a minute she thought she wasn't going to be able to pull this off. She thought she was going to laugh at her own sugary tone of voice. But then she glanced at Ty. That certainly wasn't pity in his face now!

He was severely annoyed. And the disturbing fact of the matter was that Ty Jordan annoyed was every bit as attractive as Ty Jordan not annoyed, though come to think of it, she could not remember too many times when he was not annoyed about something being out of his control.

"You put the dog in my bed? You put him there?"

"He's sick," she said, as a way of avoiding the lie without decreasing his annoyance.

"Harriet Pendleton, you are aggravation itself."

"Thank you. So you've said in the past. Don't forget, we have to be up early to get your hair right."

"You're not doing my hair again. I hate it like this. I look like an idiot and feel worse."

"Ty, it's sooo cute," she said, her voice as syrupy as sugar. If she was a man she was pretty sure she would find such a voice downright irritating.

He was looking at her narrowly, and she realized she was overplaying her part a bit and making him suspicious.

"One thing I have never had any ambition to be. Cute," he informed her dryly.

"Well, the gods can be wicked that way, give you the thing you least like."

"Really? And what did they give you?"

"Are you kidding? Everything! Great height. Not enough meat. Freckles. Buck teeth. Hair of a texture and color that no one in their right mind would ask for."

"I don't see any of those things when I look at you," he said softly.

"No?" The breathless quality to her voice would have usually made her ashamed of herself, but tonight she remembered she was trying to be annoying.

"All I see when I look at you is your...eyes."

She knew it was a lie, because he wasn't looking anywhere near her eyes. He was looking right at her lips.

"My eyes?" she stammered.

"They are the most unusual color. Mostly brown, but with flecks of gold."

He'd looked at her eyes that closely? She was going to lose all the ground she'd gained if she wasn't very careful.

Luckily, Ty seemed to catch himself. He broke the contact with her eyes, and he went and ordered the dog off the bed. Basil clenched his eyes shut and pretended to be deeply sleeping. Ty wrapped his arms around him and moved the dog, who had become a rag heap without bones, onto the floor.

"He stinks," he said, and then looked at his rumpled bed. "Damn. I suppose my bed smells just like him!" He lowered his nose to the comforter and reeled back. Whatever thoughts he had been thinking about her lips were gone. "I guess it's the couch for me tonight."

The dog yawned, stretched, and leaped back on the bed. Ty stalked from the room. When she tiptoed by the living room a few minutes later he was rolled inside an old blanket like a sausage.

"Do you need anything?" she asked, politeness itself.

Why should she feel guilty? It wasn't really her fault Basil had taken over his bed. And besides, she was going to toss and turn all night, caught in the maze of her own confused emotions. It wouldn't be fair if Ty was comfortable and happy. No, that wouldn't be fair in the least.

"Yes," he said, "I need something. I need my life back."

"Me, too," she whispered from behind her closed door. "Me, too."

Chapter Nine

He'd heard her whisper she needed her life back. She kept forgetting in a house with walls this thin, there were no secrets. So she needed her life back. And he needed his life back. Since they both wanted exactly the same thing, it seemed to him life should be very simple.

With any luck they had one day of that confounded picture taking left. The roundup in the morning, a quick drive up to snow country in the afternoon. And then—*voilà*—they had their lives back.

He told himself it was exhaustion that made him ask what was so great about his life that he'd want it back.

It was predictable, he counted firmly on the plus side.

Lord knew, nothing was predictable with Harriet in the vicinity. The mundane became an adventure, calm turned into chaos. The beat of his own heart had become unpredictable, an erratic thing. When a man could not count on his own heart to behave in a responsible manner, then it was time to take his life back.

So what if his life suddenly seemed gray and dull after a bout of sunshine?

Right now there was no sunshine. Ty didn't even feel as if he could survive until morning, let alone one more day. The couch hurt his back more than sleeping in the barn had last night. And though he ordered his mind onto other matters, it kept drifting back to the look on her face when he had come out of that pond.

When a man could not even count on his own mind to obey a simple command, then it was definitely time to take his life back.

Still, could a man imagine a look like that? Could he make up what it meant? If she cared about him that deeply, it was without a doubt the scariest thing he had ever experienced.

He took his mind off her for a few seconds by taking inventory of his scary moments. There had been that bull named Inspiration who had picked him up on his horn and tossed him ten feet in the air. There had been the time he had lost control of the truck in a blizzard and spent a freezing-cold night in the ditch. There had been the time the horse had hit a gopher hole, and he'd thought her leg was broken. He'd nearly had his arm torn off in the baler once.

He had his share of scary stuff happen.

But the truth of the matter was that for the most part it was physical scary stuff—stuff that if he pitted his brawn against it, he could usually come out, if not intact, at least the victor.

The kind of fear Harriet Pendleton was making him feel was something quite different. He could pit his brawn against it all he wanted, and it would change nothing.

She was asking him to step into uncharted territory.

Well, not asking him precisely. In fact, her words

weren't asking him at all. Her words were telling him if he fell off the face of the earth tomorrow her regret would be that they didn't have a good January picture yet.

But her mouth was telling him something different than her words. Her mouth that looked so soft and pliable. He knew what it tasted like, and so her mouth was speaking an entirely different language than her words.

Her mouth was speaking chemistry. Man–woman chemistry. And her eyes were speaking a different tune than her words, too.

Her eyes spoke to him of gentleness and a soft place to fall, of someone to talk to deep into the night. Of someone who could love him.

But there was that word again. The word he hated most in all the world. *Love.* That thing that took a man's power and rendered it completely useless. That thing that made a man helpless. All the love in the world could not stop one cell from mutating into cancer. All the love in the world could not make his own father want to live instead of die.

He heard the soft pad of footsteps, and his heart went crazy until a moist, warm tongue licked his hand.

"For God's sake," he muttered. "You already stunk up the bedroom. I don't want you in here."

The dog whined softly, turned a few circles, hitting Ty in the face with his tail each time, before he settled down on the floor. He licked Ty's hand once more.

"Okay, okay," he said grudgingly, "you can stay."

The dog's devotion unnerved him a bit. He had done nothing to deserve it. Of course, he had done nothing to deserve the light in Harriet's eyes, either.

Was love like that? Was it possible it was such a miracle that a man didn't even have to be worthy of it? That it just sought him out, showed him that his life had become desperately lonely, that he needed, after all?

He sighed. He hated philosophy of any kind. He liked hard, cold facts. Reality. Reality like the barn needed to be painted and the west quarter needed to be reseeded. Reality. Like spring calving and putting the bulls out. Reality, as in would there be enough moisture this year that he could get three thousand bales off the hayfields?

But she kept creeping into his reality check. While he counted bales, another section of his mind broke away and reminded him she was right in the next room.

Would her hair be scattered across the pillow? Would her lips be faintly parted in sleep? That other part of his mind insisted on tormenting him with the memory of her fingertips in his hair, caressing, teasing, smoothing. The other part of his mind reminded him of his own fingertips on the back of her neck after she'd been sick, and how he had been astonished by how feminine that part of her body was, how utterly and completely fragile.

"I'm driving myself crazy," he told the dog. A disciplined mind would think other thoughts. He succeeded for whole seconds at a time. He reviewed beef prices, wondered how many cows he could wean out at fifty percent of their body weight, considered his inoculation program. But as soon as he had nearly lulled himself to sleep, the guard drifted back down and it always came back to her.

And the fact she was leaving.

And he was getting his life back.

He slept only fitfully. At first light he gave up, threw on some clothes and went down to the bunkhouse where he knew Cookie would have the coffee on.

Pete and Slim were already gone, getting chores done and bringing in a few cattle for the roundup scene. He should have been pleased that they were on track with no nagging from him, but the things that made him feel pleasure seemed to be changing.

He thought of her smile. Her eyes sparkling with mischief in them. The way her jeans fit. The laughter in her voice. The softness of her lips. He nearly groaned out loud.

Cookie plunked a coffee down in front of him, and a platter of bacon and eggs just the way he liked them—the bacon very crisp, the eggs over easy. It made Ty realize something was coming, and he didn't have to wait long.

"She's lonely, you know," Cookie said.

"Who's lonely?" Ty asked, mostly to buy time since he knew darn well the only other females on the place were bovine.

"Harriet's lonely."

"She tell you that?" The bacon seemed to be turning to sawdust in his mouth. The eggs didn't taste nearly as good as they looked. They didn't have any taste at all.

When a man's breakfast lost its taste, it was one hundred percent time to take his life back.

"No! She didn't have to tell me," Cookie said. "I can just tell these things."

Cookie apparently had all sorts of skills that Ty had been happily unaware of to date. Not only did he have a personal pipeline to the Man Upstairs, he also had developed amazing sensitivity to his fellow man—make that woman—in the past few days.

"She's not lonely," Ty said firmly. "She's a big-time career woman, and she's got a full and busy life."

"People with full and busy lives are usually trying to outrun something."

Now Cookie was a philosopher.

"I have a full and busy life," Ty pointed out.

"A case in point."

"I'm not trying to outrun anything."

"Are you sure?"

Up until a few days ago, he'd been damned sure. Now, when he went to answer, not a single solitary sound came out of his mouth.

When a man's mouth refused to speak, it was time to seize back his life!

Ty studied his bacon and decided it wasn't perfect after all. Over cooked.

"She's lonely. You're lonely. Why are the two of you having so much trouble with the arithmetic?" Cookie asked stubbornly.

"Even if she was lonely, which I doubt, why would that be any of our business?"

"You could fix it."

"No, I couldn't. I can fix fences. And calves coming out the wrong way, sometimes. I can fix a field if the soil analysis tells me it needs something. I can fix a horse that has developed some bad manners. Those are things I can fix. That is the limit of my fixing ability."

"Why don't you just ask her why she's lonely?" Cookie asked.

"Because I don't think she is! Could we change the subject?"

"Okay," Cookie said. "Did you know she thinks she's ugly?"

By changing the subject, Ty had meant no more Harriet, not a shift from Harriet's loneliness to Harriet's—

"What!"

"It's true. She told me."

She really must be lonely if she was confiding her perceived inadequacies in Cookie. Somehow, her thinking she was ugly was even worse to Ty than her being lonely. Surely that would be a fairly easy thing to fix?

"So what would it hurt for you to tell her she's pretty?" Cookie said.

"Me? You tell her she's pretty."

"It wouldn't mean nothing coming from me. I'm not the world's most appealing man, as you can see."

"Neither am I."

"Humph. Nine out of ten women can't be wrong."

"Yes, they can."

"Well, only one out of ten of them counts, and she's right here on the Bar ZZ, and she thinks you're some easy to look at."

"She tell you that?" Something extraordinarily like male preening happened inside of him, to his horror.

"Maybe she didn't say it in those words, but I can tell. It would mean something coming from you if you were to just tell her she was pretty."

"Cookie?"

"Yeah, boss?"

"I don't want to talk about this anymore."

Cookie obviously had no idea how complicated the situation was. Ty wanted to kiss her day and night. She wanted to kiss him. He couldn't go telling her she was pretty without some dangerous sort of follow-up happening.

He couldn't tell her she was pretty and get his life back right on schedule.

"It's not as if your life is anything so great," Cookie muttered sulkily, refilling his coffee, slopping it over the edge of the cup so that Ty had to pull his hand out of the way hastily.

Ty glared at him. Was he able to mind read, too, the

old curmudgeon? But it was true. What was so great about his life that he was so damned anxious to get back to it?

The truth was it was familiar. Safe. There were no emotional bumps and bruises along the way. The truth was his life, for all that it was full, suddenly struck him as amazingly empty.

When had he become the kind of man who wanted safety, at any cost?

"Okay," Ty said. "I'll tell her." And let the chips fall where they may.

She came in a few minutes later, breathless, her cheeks flushed from the cool morning air. How could she think she was ugly?

"Looking mighty fine this morning," Ty said. It came out stilted and self-conscious. He could feel a tide of red moving up his neck. He hadn't blushed since he was twelve years old and Mary-Lou Blossomworth had told him her panties were pink.

Harriet stared at him. Her mouth dropped open. She blushed as deeply as he did. It occurred to him they were both equally lousy at this man–woman thing.

Not that it was a man–woman thing to tell her she looked good. He just didn't want her to go through life with the warped idea she was ugly when nothing could be further from the truth.

Watching her, standing there in the bunkhouse, looking flustered, he thought she was absolutely gorgeous. Maybe the best-looking woman he'd ever seen.

He knew nine out of ten men probably wouldn't agree with him, and he knew that wouldn't change his mind even a little bit.

She had something that others just didn't have. An authenticity of spirit.

The silence grew, she gaped at him, and then she tossed

her hair and narrowed her eyes suspiciously. Who could blame her? He was so rusty at giving a compliment that it had come out sounding stilted and entirely insincere.

He knew it would just make it worse to try and fix it. See? He had tried to tell Cookie there were some things that were not in his range of expertise when it came to fixing them. And Harriet Pendleton was definitely out of his limited range.

"Don't think that's going to get you out of the new hairdo. I brought all my stuff. Look." She held up a bag bulging with products.

She wasn't touching his hair again. He didn't care if she was lonely and if she didn't think she was pretty. Her hands in his hair was just a little more than he could handle.

"No hairstyling," he said. "That's out. It's not part of the deal."

She pouted. He saw, with sudden clarity that pouting did not come naturally to her. She was playing a game. She was trying to be a woman he would dislike.

She was trying not to be vulnerable to him.

Just the same as he was trying not to be vulnerable to her.

There was obviously no hope for them. They were both equally terrible at the man–woman thing and all its delicate nuances. It reminded him of being at a dance where he didn't know the steps.

He finished his breakfast in silence, while she chatted with Cookie. She was studiously ignoring him, which was about what he deserved. He tried not to think about how he liked her voice, and what it would be like to have a voice like that around all the time. Teasing. Playing. Talking about little things.

He got up abruptly, jammed his hat back on his head, and headed for the door.

"Don't forget the roundup," Cookie said. "I got the chuck wagon all set up at the corral."

"As if I could forget," he muttered.

"I got beans a cookin'," Cookie went on.

Harriet laughed. "You didn't really have to cook beans. You could have just put on a big pot of water. The steam coming out of it would have given the illusion you were cooking something."

Ty reminded himself that that was what she dealt in. Illusions. Except how could she be so bloody poor at the biggest illusion of all? Romance. The man–woman thing.

"Ten sharp," she called after him.

"Yeah, whatever."

The roundup went off without a hitch. The guys hammed shamelessly in the background, content, for a while, to watch as Ty roped and wrangled. Harriet got lots of shots of him heating branding irons, posing over a wriggling calf.

Apparently it was all a little too tame for his crew.

"Why don't you bulldog that big, black steer?" Pete suggested innocently.

Bulldogging, leaping from a galloping horse onto the horns of a stampeding steer and wrestling his unwilling mass to the ground was a specialized skill, and one Ty did not possess.

"Is it dangerous?" Harriet asked.

"Yes," he said.

"Nah," the three guys said in unison.

What was it about her worrying about him that made him want to leap high buildings and outrun bullets? Bulldog he did until he was so covered in dust and so sore he thought he wouldn't be able to move without hurting for a month.

But she wouldn't be here to witness that part. She only got to see the bold, daring part. He leaped from a galloping horse with a rope between his teeth and bulldogged a big mean steer and tied up his legs. He did it seven times, and he knew because he was counting.

Then the guys talked him into riding the steer. He hadn't done that sort of thing for over ten years. But what the hell? Male preening was male preening, and this was his last kick at the can.

He was still sending her away as soon as they were done, but she was going away damned impressed with the cowboy she was leaving behind.

After planting his face in the dust a dozen or so times, Ty decided being a model was downright exhausting. And not just the physical part. He did not understand this contradiction within himself that wanted to let her go, and yet was so willing to die to impress her.

Was it possible there was a word for that?

As he lay in the dust, looking at the sky, his brain completely addled and her standing over him telling him that was enough, it occurred to him there was a word for it.

He loved her. All this foolishness was about loving her.

He didn't exactly know why it had happened, or how, he just knew that it had. If a man gave in to that feeling, did his whole life become like this? Would he constantly be driving himself to new heights, to new feats of daring, to new limits of male preening?

Or did the silliness wear off after a little while?

He knew married men who didn't seem to be in a state of constant confusion and chaos. In fact, they seemed quite content.

"Ty, are you okay?"

"I don't know. I seem to have hit my head real good that time."

Maybe contentment came with surrender. He lay there, dazed, considering that possibility. But he'd never been a man to surrender. Not ever. And he only had one more day to go and he could have his life back.

He got unsteadily to his feet. They looked at each other. A powerful intensity sizzled in the air between them. It would be so easy to surrender. So much easier than fighting. He swayed toward her—

"Time to eat," Cookie called.

Lunch tasted like sawdust, the very same way breakfast had, even though it was real chuck wagon fare, and he usually loved it.

"So who's all coming up to the snow country?" Ty asked, when lunch was done. He was aware of the clock ticking. Snow pictures, and then they were done.

"I will," Pete said.

Ty didn't miss the sharp kick he received from Cookie.

"On second thought, I have some stuff to do this afternoon."

"Me, too," Slim said, catching on rapidly.

"So, it's just the two of us," Ty said grimly. Was she as aware as he was of his guys shamelessly matchmaking? That they had caught the current passing between the two and were aiding and abetting it?

"Three," she said. "Basil's coming, aren't you baby?"

Baby seemed to have made a complete recovery. He wiggled ecstatically at being spoken to. Still, Ty realized he had better be nice to the dog.

The dog was staying. She was leaving.

This was the pathetic truth about his life: he was going to keep the dog and let her go.

"Huh?"

"Snow clothes," she repeated. "Do you have a wool hat?"

He was throwing his snow clothes in the truck when Cookie came up the path to the house, struggling under the weight of a huge wicker basket.

"I didn't know how long you two would be, so I packed a few things for you."

It was romance in a basket, Ty could see that at a glance. There was a bottle of wine in there for God's sake!

"Where did you get a basket like that?" Ty asked, annoyed.

"Stacey give it to me last year for Christmas. It had the nice little jars of jam in it and the specialty coffees."

"I don't think we need a picnic supper," Ty said. "You fed us enough for lunch."

"It wouldn't hurt you to woo her a bit. Make her feel pretty."

"I don't know how to woo people," Ty said in an undertone. "And what would the point be? She is leaving. As soon as these pictures are done, she is getting back in her little car and going back to her life."

"You could stop her."

"I don't want to stop her, Cookie. I want her to go."

Cookie looked at him sadly. "Then you're a fool, Ty Jordan. I ain't seen you so alive for many, many years."

It was true. He felt aggravated nearly all the time. He felt as though his life was upside down and backward. He felt as if his heart was a traitor within his own chest.

But Lordy, he did feel alive.

What was it going to be like to go back to sleep-walking after this? Grudgingly he took the basket from Cookie.

"Don't get any ideas," he said. "She's not staying."

But Cookie was grinning ear-to-ear, as if he had said the exact opposite. "Oh, and here's the barrel I made for around Basil's neck. It looks pretty good, don't it?"

It looked like a bleach bottle on a string, but Ty didn't say anything, just set the prop in with the rest of the items.

She arrived a few minutes later, looking hilarious in too many clothes. He let himself smile. What the heck? He was close to the finish line now. He could take a few chances. He could give himself over to just enjoying her. How much damage could that do in just a few hours?

It seemed to him that decision to just go with it, instead of fighting it, changed everything. Even the color of the sky seemed to be a deeper blue.

He allowed himself to be drawn into her enjoyment of the landscape as they took the twisting road that would eventually snake them up the mountain into snow.

"Ty," she said suddenly, "how come you aren't in a relationship?"

See you let your guard down, and in came the sucker punch.

"No opportunity," he said. "I don't get out much. I don't have time. How am I supposed to meet anyone?"

"Do you think it might be because of your mom and dad?"

He threw her a glance. This was really the road he least wanted to go down with her.

"Do you think losing them might have made you wary of relationships?"

"Harriet, I don't know. Can't we talk about horses?"

"No," she said stubbornly.

He recognized now that it was a hostage taking. He was stuck in a truck with her for at least an hour. And she wanted to talk about deep things. Personal things.

Things he'd been holding inside for his whole damned life.

"You know why I'm not married?" he said. "Because my mom died when I was seventeen and my dad a year later. I was seventeen years old and I had a kid to raise. Once that was done, once Stacey was grown up, I'd had my fill of responsibility."

"So, why didn't you sell the ranch and go on a trip around the world? If you'd had enough of responsibility? You could have been a beach bum in California for a few years, or a ski instructor in the Swiss Alps."

Despite himself he laughed. "I guess I never thought of it," he said.

"Or maybe you got addicted to being responsible. In charge of everybody and everything. Totally in control."

"Nothing wrong with a little control," he said. "Look, we're coming into some snow." He hoped it would distract her. "We'll have to be careful, though. Do you see that bank there? How the snow is trickling down it in little balls no bigger than a pea? That means the snow is real soft. It's an avalanche warning. We'll have to stick to flat ground."

Apparently avalanches did not concern her in the least.

"You know what I think? I think you love people too deeply. I bet raising Stacey was pure hell for you. I bet you worried nonstop and felt like the world was going to end every time she went out the door."

He stared straight ahead. It was a little spooky how close that was to the truth. Being Stacey's parent had been totally nerve-racking. He had hated all the moments of pure helplessness involved in looking after her, he had hated all those moments when he had had to let her go.

Maybe he had even decided, deep inside himself, he

wasn't strong enough to do it all again, with kids of his own.

"Love doesn't have to be like that," she said softly.

He said nothing.

"Stacey was a child. You wouldn't feel that way with a full-grown woman. Maybe what you need is someone to share the load with you, instead of carrying it all yourself."

Only a few more hours and he could be out of this, safe and sound. If he steeled himself to the longing her words created in him.

He had a picture of them, vivid and compelling, together. Coming home to Harriet at night. Sharing the load. Not being lonely anymore.

"This looks like great snow," he said, slammed the truck into gear and set the brake. He hopped out.

The snow was spring snow, soft and sticky. The sky was brilliant blue. He remembered the storyboard and began a snowball. In a few moments it was huge.

She tucked away the camera and came and pushed it with him. Their shoulders kept slipping and touching. She didn't look like a very strong woman, and yet he was amazed at how much easier it was to share the load.

And he was amazed how much fun it was. How long since he had done something this foolishly carefree as building a snowman?

Their laughter rang up the mountain. Basil galloped around them, burrowing in snow, coming up with it all over his face. They threw snowballs for him to catch, laughed until their stomachs hurt when he would catch the snowball and then be baffled when it broke into smithereens. He would chase around looking frantically for it.

She took pictures of him playing with the dog, and

pictures of him throwing snowballs. He felt like a young boy.

Finally, when they were exhausted, he took the basket out of the back seat. There was even a blanket in there, and he spread it on the snow.

"You want wine?" he said, and then felt embarrassed, as if she might suspect him of wooing her.

"No, thanks. Is there hot chocolate?"

Somehow he was glad she wasn't a wine kind of girl. But then maybe that was part of the control thing. Wine would be a terrible part of the equation up here if he wanted to keep control.

Or the little bit of control that he had.

It seemed to him that, somewhere along the way, the whole afternoon had slipped from his control. And that he was glad. That it felt good. That the world did not, after all, quit spinning when he was not in charge of it.

They sat on the blanket and sipped hot chocolate and ate the thick sandwiches that Cookie had prepared.

And then he made the fatal error. He said, "We've talked enough about me. Now I want to know about you."

"And what do you want to know?"

"I want to know why you aren't in a relationship."

"You know, Ty, I'm just like you. I thought it was because I lacked opportunity, and I thought it was because the opposite sex didn't find me attractive, and I thought it was because I was a complete washout sexually, and I thought my brief and disastrous marriage had made me wary for all time."

"And now?"

She looked at him, her eyes so clear he could see straight to her soul.

And she said softly, "And now I know it's because I fell in love with a man a long, long time ago. I gave him my heart, and I never took it back."

Chapter Ten

Harriet closed her eyes, took a deep breath and then opened them again, and looked directly at Ty. She felt courage, emotional courage, long slumbering within her, stir to life.

It was the moment of truth. All these years she'd been trying to get over the fact she had fallen in love with a lonesome cowboy when she was too young and inexperienced to know better. All these years she had tried to move on, to minimize, to rationalize, to get over it as if it was an illness.

What if she had given as much effort to pursuing what her heart had been trying to tell her as she had to running away?

Her problem was not what she had always thought it was. It wasn't that she wasn't pretty enough. The problem wasn't that she was too skinny and too freckled and too bucktoothed and too tall.

The problem was not that she was accident prone or clumsy or that disaster followed in her wake.

The problem was that she had not been brave. Four years ago, when she was younger and more naive, perhaps it had been forgivable that she never told this man how she felt, that she had let her feelings of inadequacy drive her away from taking a risk on her own heart and her own happiness.

Looking at it now she saw how loving Ty had shaped her in many ways. Ty had made her want to be more than she was: more beautiful, more accomplished, more successful, more worthy.

Loving him had driven her in a frenzy of proving herself, accumulating experiences and successes the way other women accumulated jewelry and outfits.

Even marrying Zorro had been about Ty. *See world? A handsome man can love me. I am worthy.*

And the problem was, up until this point, she had somehow always seen love as being about her getting something, filling the hole inside her that said she wasn't good enough. Wouldn't love make her feel, finally, that she was all right? That she measured up?

But suddenly, in the clear, crisp mountain air, with Ty beside her, she saw how wrong she had been. Her loving Ty wasn't about *getting*. Not if it was real. If it was real, it would be about giving something to him.

Ty was alone in his strength, and she could take some of the load from his shoulders. Ty, fiercely independent, had not learned that sharing could make life richer and fuller than his wildest dreams.

He was too rigid, and she could give him the gift of spontaneity. He was too serious, and she could give him the gift of laughter.

He was so wrapped up in the mechanics of getting through each day that he had forgotten how to live. He had forgotten how to slow down, breathe deep, relax, have fun.

And the irony would be that with each gift she gave him, Harriet would receive everything she had ever dreamed of or hoped for.

Not telling him how she felt when love had first stirred in her soul for her best friend's brother had given her something else. She knew, so much better than other young women her age, where her happiness was not.

It was not in seeing the world, in accumulating successes, in attaining material wealth. It was not in having her eyes and teeth fixed and her hair done.

Harriet took another deep breath. She tossed the dice of her life right at his feet. She picked up his hand and touched it to her lips. And with every ounce of courage she possessed, she said, "The man I gave my heart to was you."

His jaw dropped, and his eyes widened. He scanned her face, then swallowed hard. For just a moment she felt him lean toward the gift, drawn by its warmth. For just a moment she felt him give in to the power of what was being offered. For just a moment she felt what she had never dreamed plain-Jane Harriet Pendleton could feel.

She felt irresistible.

Then he pulled back, and yanked his hand away from her as though she'd bitten him. "Me?" he croaked. "You gave your heart to me? All those years ago, when you were here?"

She nodded uncertainly.

"Harriet, that was a dumb thing to do."

She wasn't sure what she had expected. Shock, yes, but she had rather hoped shock would give way to delighted surprise, and quickly, too! She had rather hoped he would recognize that he needed her as much as *she* recognized it.

He was staring at her as if he had never seen her before. Then he looked away and took a deep breath, scanning the snow-covered mountains as if he would find answers written on the craggy peaks.

She followed his gaze and looked up at the sun hitting the snowcapped mountain above them. So, she had risked it all.

And lost.

Harriet, that was a dumb thing to do. What an insulting reaction to such a heartfelt declaration of love. What had she expected? When had anything in her whole life ever gone the way she had expected? Why was she so surprised that even her declaration of love was a disaster?

Still, she decided bravely, perhaps knowing she had lost was better than living out her days in limbo. In a detached sort of way, she noticed she did not regret the risk she had taken. She would not take the words back, even if she could turn back the clock.

She got shakily to her feet. Obviously, she had made Ty completely miserable. Embarrassed him. Left him without words.

"Come on, Basil," she said, "let's go for a walk."

"Harriet—"

"No. Don't feel like you have to say anything. I read you loud and clear."

"I don't think you do," he said, getting to his feet. He moved to take her hand but she shifted it away, proudly.

He was going to tell her how flattered he was. And how undeserving of her love. And that he would always like her as a friend. Gee. She'd heard those words a few times in high school and in college. Silence was preferable to that. To his pity or kindness.

"Harriet, I—"

She held up her hand. "It'll have to wait. I have an emergency."

He scowled. What kind of emergency could she have after all?

"The ladies' room?" she said sweetly.

He actually turned red. She watched with interest as the tide moved up the broad column of his neck into his face. She congratulated herself on having found the perfect way to terminate the conversation.

On the other hand, his reaction was the type of thing that made her fall for him in the first place—that underneath all that masculine strength and bravado was a man endearingly sweet, without defenses, without armor.

"Pick a tree," he said uncomfortably.

"Come on, Basil," she said.

"Don't go far," he said. "Remember what I said about the snow. It's soft. It's unstable at this time of year."

It occurred to her an avalanche would make a nice diversion at the moment. Nothing like a little disaster to help people through an awkward moment.

"So much the better if it buried me," she muttered to Basil. "A tragic and dramatic end. I bet Ty Jordan would hate himself for the rest of his life."

Childish, of course, to think such thoughts.

Of course, she didn't pay the least bit of attention to him or his warnings about the snow. She just needed to be away from him and fast, to be by herself, to say goodbye to the hope of him ever loving her back, once and for all.

So she wasn't really paying attention when she heard the first small rumble. But then she noticed the tiny little trickle of pebble-size snowballs coming down the snowy slope she was skirting.

"I was kidding," she said out loud to Fate. But apparently Fate was not in a joking mood. To her horror, a wall of snow, foaming like a huge cresting wave, was moving toward her, more swiftly than could be believed.

Denial and disbelief froze her to the spot.

She was going to die. And Ty probably was going to be sorry. He'd blame himself, and think over the words they had exchanged, over and over—looking, too late, for the words that would have kept her on the blanket.

And then she felt how deep her love for him was, because she would have done anything to prevent him the agony of regret. In the last moment, before the snow hit, her thoughts were not of herself and of her mortality but of Ty. She wished she could have just a second more, to tell him it wasn't his fault, to tell him she forgave him.

The wall of snow and Basil hit her nearly simultaneously, Basil maybe a fraction of a second before the snow. She felt his enormous weight push her, throw her to one side, but it was not quite enough.

Then Harriet was enveloped in an icy wave, tumbled mercilessly until she did not know if she was up or down, backward or forward. Her body rolled itself into a ball. Aside from the roaring in her ears, she could have been inside a ruthlessly shaken bottle of milk.

The motion stopped as abruptly as it had began. Her immediate reaction of relief was short-lived. She became aware of a terrible silence. And of a crushing weight all around her, as if she was trapped in concrete. It was black in this prison. And very cold. Terror swept her when she was unable to move any of her limbs. She could not even wiggle her fingers.

She had been buried alive.

Terror gave way, slowly, to resignation. And then a hint of gratitude pierced her icy prison. She could breathe.

There must be an air pocket where her nose was tucked nearly in against her chest.

Stuck and desperate, Harriet made the happy discovery that even if Ty didn't love her, she still wanted to live. She realized, somehow and somewhere, she had come to love herself enough to get through this matter of the heart. If she survived.

Maybe that was part of why she had not said anything to Ty on her first visit to the Bar ZZ. Her soul had known she would have to be whole to love someone else. Sure of herself and her own competence.

Of course, she might have appreciated the universal plan better had Ty said yes instead of rejected her.

Feeling strangely drowsy, Harriet contemplated all the gifts loving him had given her. From the very start, hadn't falling in love with Ty Jordan made her more than she was before? Had she not felt deeper, a richness of soul, a compassion for all living things that she had not so consciously felt before? Loving him had, simply, made her better.

She realized loving Ty had given her a different way of seeing and interpreting the world around her. The song he had put in her heart all those years ago had sung on, even when he was not there.

The song had been in every picture she had ever taken.

Love had put beauty in her soul, and that had become her gift to give the world. She hoped she would survive to give that gift some more, but she felt oddly at ease.

A sense of total surrender came over her. And with it an all-encompassing sensation of peace.

And then, muted, distant, she heard the dog barking. She held her breath to hear better, and could hear scratching, the scrabble of his claws on hard, packed snow.

"Let Ty be with him. Please, God."

Then she heard his voice, a deep rumble. Calling. Over and over again. Her name. His voice, the sounds of digging, became clearer.

She called back until her voice was hoarse.

The weight lifted from around her, little by little. Light began to permeate the darkness. And when the sun burst through and touched her face, she smiled. She had gone to Heaven after all.

Because it looked just like Ty leaning over her, digging away. And every time he looked at her, she saw the truth.

All the masks gone from his eyes, all the protective layers stripped away.

Yes, she had made Heaven.

Because he loved her back. And he couldn't hide it.

"Hang in there, Harriet," he said tenderly. "Almost free. Almost free. Don't panic. Don't worry. I've got you. I'm going to look after you."

So that was what Heaven felt like. A light inside of you, so brilliant you felt too small to hold it.

"Forever. You hear me?" His voice was strong and tender, soothing, but she could see fear in his eyes. "I'm going to look after you forever. You need me. How have you managed to survive this long without me looking out for you? Me and Basil that is."

Basil licked her face in confirmation. She could not move away from him. And she could not even laugh at how alive the warm roughness of his tongue on her cheek made her feel.

"Okay. Your head is out, and your neck, most of your chest. No broken bones so far. Nothing at all to worry about."

She knew Ty was keeping up the patter of chatter to keep her calm. It was just like last time, when she'd fallen off the horse.

She tried to tell him it was different this time. She wasn't scared, and she didn't feel any pain. She tried to tell him she was calm, but when she tried to open her mouth to speak it seemed like the effort was too great.

When he dug carefully around her arm, and she felt it free, she tried to reach up, to touch his face, but her arm wouldn't move. She commanded it again, to reach up, but the arm did nothing.

"Harriet, don't even try to move."

He was always so bossy. She wanted to touch his face. She could move if she wanted to. He was going to have to learn not to boss her around. She felt him brush the last of the snow from her other arm.

The whole upper part of her body was free. She reached over to help the arm that wasn't working.

She tugged on it.

The pain exploded in her head. And then the dazzling white all around her, the light in his eyes, and the white of his teeth, and the sun sparking off the snow, they all swirled briefly, and then dissolved into total darkness.

Through the darkness she heard him calling her name, but she could not answer him. And then even that was gone.

She was floating. No, she was flying. A woman loved, cherished. Harriet, buried up to her waist in snow, trapped, felt as safe and warm and happy as she had ever felt in her entire life. She supposed that was a miracle.

The pain tried to come back, but she shoved it away, staying right where she was, in this healing place where love washed over her.

But finally the pain called her back so intensely that she could not move away from it. It hurt to open her eyes. Her arm hurt, her head hurt, her whole body ached. Her mouth felt like she had been eating sand.

Through the haze of pain, Harriet was startled to see that she was not on a snow-covered mountain. Straight above her head was acoustic tile. She could smell disinfectant. She was tucked tightly into crisp white sheets. She was in the hospital.

"Where's Basil?" she cried, coming awake.

"Basil?" a deep voice responded, laced with weariness. "I should be insulted."

Even though it hurt to turn her head, she did it anyway. Even though it hurt to smile, nothing could have stopped her.

"I knew you were here," she whispered. "Could feel you. Feel your spirit."

He took her hand gently. "Go back to sleep. You're going to be all right. I'm not leaving you. Not ever."

"My head hurts."

"A few tons of snow tends to have that effect."

"And my arm," she whispered.

"Broken in three places. How am I supposed to make a cowgirl out of you when you have bird bones that break so easy?" He held the glass of water, adjusted the straw between her lips.

"Is Basil okay?"

"He's never been better."

"What about my camera?"

"It didn't make it."

"All the winter shots," she said mournfully. "They were good, too."

"Harriet, not now for God's sake. We have all kinds of time to do the winter shots. We can rent the snow-blowing machine from the ski hill if we have to."

"But you want to get rid of me, don't you?" she asked, confused. "I'm on a schedule, right? What day is it?"

"Harriet, you're never getting rid of me. You're stuck

with me. You've got all the rest of your life to take pictures of my sweet mug.''

She frowned. ''No, because you said it was dumb to fall in love with you.''

''Well, from my perspective any woman who would fall for a barely socialized, set-in-his-ways, basic type-A, I've-gotta-control-the-world personality, is a bit on the dumb side. But now that you have, I intend to make the best of it.''

''That's why you said it was dumb? Not because I was being hopeless? Not because you could never love a girl like me back?''

''Oh, Harriet,'' he said tenderly. ''You move so damn quick. You told me you loved me and then hopped up and ran away before I even knew what to do with what you'd given me.''

''You weren't going to reject me?''

''I might have tried. For your own good. I have faults. I don't think you're fully aware of what you are taking on. I'm nearly scared to death of love.

''But then near-death showed me I was way more scared not to love. In those minutes when I thought I had lost you, my whole world exploded. Not one thing that I had thought mattered before that avalanche still mattered after. Well, one thing still mattered. You.''

''I thought I wasn't appealing enough. You know, not pretty. Not particularly feminine. Not someone who's going to sew buttons on your shirts. Not somebody who is going to take orders from you.''

''You know what I think, Harriet? You were a cute little duckling, not an ugly one. And you missed your own transformation into a swan. I wonder how long it will take me to get you to see yourself as I see you and as you really are? Longer, if I'm not allowed to give orders, I guess."

She smiled at him. "This is the nicest dream I've ever had." She closed her eyes and drifted, felt his hand on her forehead and then his lips.

"Don't feel guilty," she whispered. "I couldn't bear it if you were only being nice because you felt guilty."

"The only thing I feel guilty about is wasting so much time. Dumb cowboy like me. It takes an avalanche to shake my feelings out of me."

She snorted. "Don't make me laugh," she pleaded. "Are you sure Basil is okay?"

"Oh, never better. Cookie is feeding him T-bone steaks and the local news crew came out and did a feature on him. He finally made the grade. A real live rescue dog. People are coming out of the woodwork wanting to give him homes."

"You're giving Basil away?"

"Nah. He's got a home, forever. And all the T-bone he can eat. He saved your life, Harriet, plain and simple. He pushed you out of the main path of the snow, and then he showed me right where you were buried."

She looked at Ty's face more closely. With the dark shadows of whiskers on his cheeks and chin, he should have looked like a renegade, like a complete outlaw. But he didn't. He looked different than she had ever seen him look before, some guard gone from his eyes, some softness around his mouth.

"Am I on drugs?" she asked.

"Yes, ma'am."

"Because I just love the whole world so much. And you so much. And Basil, too. And Pete and Slim and Cookie."

"That's a relief that you love the old reprobates. Because when you marry me, they come with the package. It's like inheriting evil stepchildren, I know, but there's nothing I can do about it.''

"When I marry you?" she stammered.

"Go back to sleep, love. I'm saving the proposal for when you're not all doped up.''

"I propose we give the dog a medal," she said tiredly.

"That's exactly why I'm not saying anything else of importance to you right now, Miss Morphine.''

"That's worse than Lady Disaster. Miss Morphine." She giggled and then giggled again. "Do you love me, Ty? Really and truly?''

"I'll divulge that one important thing right now. I love you, Harriet.''

"I sure like this dream," she said again, and floated away on the beautiful white swan that swam by. She called back to him, "I love you, too.''

The next time she woke up, the sun was streaming through the slats in the Venetian blinds, making stripes across her bed. At first the silence made her think she was alone, but she heard a faint stirring and turned her head.

Ty was fast asleep in the chair beside the bed, his long legs stretched out in front of him. His cowboy hat was tilted over his face, but she could still see the whiskers darkening his cheeks and his jaws, the exhausted pallor on his skin, the dark crescents under his eyes.

He looked like hell.

"Cute, huh?" a nurse said, coming in and glancing over at him.

Only Ty Jordan could look the way he did in this moment, and still elicit that comment.

"Adorable," Harriet agreed. He frowned, not liking the term, even asleep.

"How are you feeling?" the nurse asked. "You are one

lucky girl. I've seen people come in from head-on colli-
sions that don't look as banged up as you did when you
got here. You're very lucky to be alive.''

"I know," Harriet said, and meant it.

"He's been here for three days," the nurse said, nodding at Ty. "Normally we would have thrown him out,
but the nurses can't resist him."

"Nine out of ten can't be wrong," Harriet said with a
smile.

"What's that?"

"Oh, nothing. I'll be sending you a shipment of calendars to sell for me in a few months, though. Starring
him."

"Those should sell themselves," the nurse said.

"That was the general idea."

"The other three cowboys keep coming by. They've
brought Mr. Jordan fresh clothes. They tried to smuggle
the dog in once. They track dirt in the halls, and two of
them chew. Nurse Hendricks nearly has them trained,
though." The nurse leaned closer. "Just between you and
me, I think she's got her eye on Cookie."

"Really?" Harriet said, delighted.

"Oh, there's romance in the air. Especially in this
room. Mr. Jordan's devoted to you," the nurse said with
an envious little smile. "I've been a nurse for a long time.
He's pretty special."

"I know."

"He was rehearsing his proposal in the hall the other
day."

"He was?"

"And let me tell you something, girl, don't say no. He
wouldn't even get out the door without being snagged by
someone else. Nurse Hendricks is on the hunt."

"I'm not saying no," Harriet said.

"Good," a gruff, sleep-roughened voice said. "That'll save me the trouble of asking."

"Not to mention the trouble of staving off Nurse Hendricks," the nurse said with a wink and a grin before she left them alone.

"You know," he said, waking and stretching, "you think you're this big, rough-and-tumble cowboy who knows the meaning of the word *tough*. And then you find out *tough* is finding the right words to convince a woman she should spend the rest of her life on you."

"Try me," she invited.

"All right. Harriet, I'm a rough-spoken, hard-living cowboy with no education to speak of. You can dance circles around me in the smarts department. Nothing I've done has made me worthy of asking you to marry me, but if you'd overlook my flaws and have me anyway, I'd be the happiest man on earth."

"You know, Ty, I finally figured it out. Maybe love isn't about being worthy. Maybe it's just about being enough for one other person in the whole world. You're enough for me. Just the way you are."

"So that's yes, right?"

She smiled. "Right."

"I had to look through your purse when we brought you in, to see if there was a number for anyone we should call. A relative or something. I called your mom and your sister. They've been in and out."

"Thanks. That will save us the awkward family dinner since you've already met."

"I found this, Harriet." He took it carefully from his front shirt pocket and laid it on her stomach.

She looked at what he had put there, and her eyes filled with tears.

It was one of the photos she had taken of him, four

years ago, when Stacey had unwittingly played her part in a meeting destined to be.

He was sitting on a paint horse, his posture relaxed, his cowboy hat pulled low and the collar of his slicker up high. He looked like the quintessential romantic hero.

"What was I smiling at?" he asked.

Harriet smiled. "Me. You thought my devotion to my first camera was endlessly amusing. I had dropped it, and I was down in the dirt wiping it off as if I'd dropped a baby. I looked up and you had that look on your face— that little tender smile. And I took the picture."

"It's the one that won the contest, isn't it, Harriet?"

She nodded, stroked the worn surface of the photo with loving fingers. "Yes."

"Now, you see, that's something of a relief to me."

"It is?"

"Yup. Because nine out of ten women didn't vote for me, Harriet."

"But—"

He touched his fingertip to her lips, silencing her. And then he lowered his head and kissed her.

It was a kiss that was sweet and welcoming and held the promise of a thousand tomorrows and the passions of a thousand years gone by.

"They voted for this," he said, tracing her lips with his tongue. "Love. They saw the pure love shining in that picture, and they voted for that.

"For love and for hope and for innocence and for all the things that are good in this world. It isn't really a picture of me at all, Harriet. It's a picture of you."

The tears came silently at first, and then turned into great racking sobs. He climbed right into the bed with her, ever so gently lifted her bruised body onto his lap.

He rocked her against him, held her tight, until the tears

were done and all that was left was the contented joy of a woman who knew that all her life she had been waiting for someone to see her.

And finally someone had.

Epilogue

"Look," Ty said into the phone, "I don't care how much money you want to give me. There's nothing I want that money can buy. Yeah, well, same to you."

He flopped back on the bed, threw his arm over his forehead.

Harriet kissed the curve of his biceps. "It'll die down," she said. "You'll see."

The phone rang.

"If you answer that, I'm divorcing you," Ty said.

She rolled her eyes, climbed over him and looked at the call display. "It's your sister. Not a movie company. Not a modeling agency."

"Somebody's gotten to her," he said cynically. "Just you wait. She'll have some proposal she's pushing. I can't stand much more of this."

"The phone company says our new number will be in on Monday," she said soothingly, and picked up the phone. "She probably phoned to wish me a happy birthday. Hello, Stacey. Thanks. What did Ty give me? He was just giving me my present right now.''

Ty kissed her neck.

"What else did I get? Cookie gave me a cookbook. I think he's trying to get us ready for something. Kathy Hendricks, the nurse, comes out here and rides with him once or twice a week.''

Ty took her earlobe in between his teeth and nibbled, then nipped.

"A calendar for next year? Stacey, right now might not be the best time to talk about it.''

Ty snatched the phone from her. "Never would be a good time to talk about it. Never. What do you mean calm down? And it's none of your business what we're doing. What do you mean you know exactly what we're doing? I'm hanging up now. Thirty seconds? Okay, but I'm looking at my watch.''

He glared at his watch for thirty seconds and then, without saying goodbye, hung up.

"I think you may be crankier than ever,'' Harriet said, and touched his bottom lip with her tongue.

"I have important things on my mind,'' he said huskily, "and I'm in no mood to be interrupted.''

They had been married four months. The truth was neither of them was ever in any mood to be interrupted.

"Stacey wants to do another calendar. For the Breast Cancer Research Foundation again,'' he said into her ear.

"Not starring my husband,'' she said firmly, just in case he was considering it.

"Well, actually she didn't want me for it.''

"She didn't?''

He was laughing now. "They want Basil. People are crazy about the dog. He's getting fan mail from little kids.

"She's actually already worked out a concept. She

wants to do a calendar called Baby and the Beast. Something about Basil with a baby crawling all over him.''

''I think we could lend her Basil for that.''

''She wants you to do the photography.''

''That sounds like fun.''

''I have an idea that sounds like even more fun. We could keep the whole thing in the family. All we'd have to do is come up with a baby.''

''This is getting more fun by the second,'' she said, slipping her tongue around the edge of his lip.

When he came up for air, he said, ''Then again, I think maybe I just want my son or daughter to be a regular kid. No modeling for calendars. Stacey can come up with her own baby.''

''Does that mean you're softening toward the hippie?''

''He got his hair cut,'' Ty said grudgingly. ''He's got a pretty good job, for a hippie. Besides, they've been married nearly as long as us.''

''And that's long enough to know when you should be talking and when you should be kissing,'' Harriet told him.

''Yes, ma'am,'' he said.

*   *   *   *   *

If you enjoyed what you just read,
then we've got an offer you can't resist!

Take 2 bestselling love stories FREE!
Plus get a FREE surprise gift!

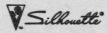

SPECIAL EDITION™

Was it something in the water...
or something in the air?

Because bachelors in Bridgewater, Texas,
are becoming a vanishing breed—fast!

**Don't miss these three exciting stories of Texas
cowboys by favorite author Jodi O'Donnell:**

Deke Larrabie returns to discover
someone *else* he left behind....
THE COME-BACK COWBOY
(Special Edition #1494)
September 2002

Connor Brody meets his match and gives her
THE RANCHER'S PROMISE
(Silhouette Romance #1619)
October 2002

Griff Corbin learns about true
friendship and love when he falls for
HIS BEST FRIEND'S BRIDE
(Silhouette Romance #1625)
November 2002

Available at your favorite retail outlet.

Where love comes alive™

SILHOUETTE Romance

COMING NEXT MONTH

#1618 THE WILL TO LOVE—Lindsay McKenna
Morgan's Mercenaries: Ultimate Rescue
With her community destroyed by an earthquake, Deputy Sheriff
Kerry Chelton turned to Sergeant Quinn Grayson to help establish order
and rebuild. But when Kerry was injured, Quinn began to realize that no
devastation compared to losing Kerry....

#1619 THE RANCHER'S PROMISE—Jodi O'Donnell
Bridgewater Bachelors
Lara Dearborn's new boss was none other than Connor Brody—the
son of her sworn enemy! Connor had worked his entire life to escape
Mick Brody's legacy. But could he have a future with Lara when the
truth about their fathers came out?

#1620 FOR THE TAKING—Lilian Darcy
A Tale of the Sea
Thalassa Morgan wanted to put the past behind her, something that Lou-
can—claimant of the Pacifica throne—wouldn't allow. Reluctantly she
returned to Pacifica as his wife to restore order to their kingdom. But
her sexy, uncompromising husband proved to be far more dangerous
than the nightmares haunting her....

#1621 CROWNS AND A CRADLE—Valerie Parv
The Carramer Legacy
She thought she'd won a vacation to Carramer—but discovered her
true identity! Sarah McInnes's grandfather was Prince Henry Valmont—
and her one-year-old son the royal heir! Now, handsome, intense Prince
Josquin had to persuade her to stay—but were his motives political or
personal?

#1622 THE BILLIONAIRE'S BARGAIN—Myrna Mackenzie
The Wedding Auction
What does a confirmed bachelor stuck caring for his eighteen-month-
old twin brothers do? Buy help from a woman auctioning her services
for charity! But beautiful April Pruitt was no ordinary nanny, and
Dylan Valentine wondered if his bachelorhood was the next item on
the block!

#1623 THE SHERIFF'S 6-YEAR-OLD SECRET—Donna Clayton
The Thunder Clan
Nathan Thunder avoided intimate relationships—and discovering he had
an independent six-year-old daughter wasn't going to change that!
Gwen Fleming wanted to help her teenage brother. Could two mis-
matched families find true love?

Visit Silhouette at www.eHarlequin.com